RANGER KU-043-723

Sent by the dying Captain McNelly to investigate the power-crazy Earl Solomon, Texas Ranger Brad Saunders is soon out of his depth, struggling to defend a bank . . . Enter Lieutenant Lee Hall, McNelly's successor, who has vastly different ideas on upholding the law. With Hall's arrival, Brad finds himself battling at the sharp end of a new order, where outlaws reach the end of the road not at the point of a smoking gun — but dangling on a rope . . .

D. A. HORNCASTLE

RANGER LAW

Complete and Unabridged

LINFORD
Leicester

First published in Great Britain in 1995 by
Robert Hale Limited
London

First Linford Edition
published 2002
by arrangement with
Robert Hale Limited
London

British Library CIP Data

Horncastle, D. A.
    Ranger law.—Large print ed.—
Linford western library
1. Western stories
2. Large type books
I. Title
823.9'14 [F]

ISBN 0–7089–9803–8

Published by
F. A. Thorpe (Publishing)
Anstey, Leicestershire
Set by Words & Graphics Ltd.
Anstey, Leicestershire
Printed and bound in Great Britain by
T. J. International Ltd., Padstow, Cornwall

This book is printed on acid-free paper

For Julie

1

'Captain McNelly will see you now.'

Fiddling nervously with his hat, Brad Saunders rose to follow the nurse in her crisply starched uniform along the airy corridors of the sanatorium. She paused at the door to a private room.

'Captain McNelly is far from well,' she said in a low voice. 'So don't stay long, if you please.'

Brad nodded as he cautiously opened the door. There was no arguing with nurses. Hospitals always made him feel strangely vulnerable — he had the healthy man's instinctive abhorrence of the sickroom. Illness of this kind unnerved him. He'd seen enough of life to know that a quick death from a bullet was infinitely preferable to the lingering ending endured by the acute consumptive. This disease, the incurable scourge of the times, made no distinction between its victims. And the puzzle of it was that a vigorous, outdoor man like Captain McNelly was just as vulnerable as a pallid young woman languishing in a salon back east.

Captain Leander H. McNelly, commander of the Special Force, Texas Rangers, lay propped against his pillows. His hair was combed and his beard neatly trimmed. Even in his sick-bed, he maintained the same high standards he set for himself and expected of his men.

As Brad moved forward to shake hands he was shocked at the profound change wrought in the man since he had last seen him. The skin of the previously bronzed forehead was pale as parchment and the fingers almost skeletal as he grasped them. The effort of shaking hands brought on an acute fit of coughing, every bark of which drew Brad's spirits lower. It was plain that Captain McNelly had forked his last saddle.

It seemed like an age before McNelly could speak.

2

'First of all, Brad, the State Governor has asked me to pass on his personal thanks for the job you did in exposing that counterfeit money racket. You did a good job there.' McNelly smiled as he spoke. Although physically weak, his voice still carried the incisive authority of a man who had risen to be a company commander in the Confederate Army at the age of eighteen.

'Maybe I was a mite lucky,' Brad said, embarrassedly, still twiddling with his hat. He badly wanted to smoke but a large notice strictly forbade it.

'That's not the way I see it,' McNelly said. 'You're too modest, Brad. You're a damn good ranger, a credit to the finest company of men I've ever been entrusted to command. I'm making you up to sergeant forthwith.'

Brad swallowed hard. 'But Cap'n . . . '

'No buts . . . that's my decision and I have to tell you, Brad, there won't be any more. I know the score, the medics are very cagey but they can't keep it from me. I know I haven't got much longer to live. That apart, all the medical treatment is a big strain on the company's finances. I'm gonna have to give way to someone else quite soon.'

McNelly's body was racked again with a hollow, dry, barking cough. As Brad waited for the paroxysm to pass, he looked at his frail captain with mixed feelings of compassion and anger as he pondered the great mystery that has baffled mankind since the Creation: why was it that the best were always taken and the worst 'flourished like the green bay tree' — as McNelly himself had once so eloquently put it.

'I didn't bring you here just to congratulate you,' McNelly said when he had recovered. 'I've got a job for you.'

'Anything you say, Cap'n,' Brad said — and he meant it. He'd follow this man to hell and back, he didn't have to ask.

A flicker of a smile graced the sick captain's lips.

'You're a loner, Brad. I knew that from the day I first met you. I know rank means nothing to you, but it'll help place you in the eyes of your new captain when he's appointed. My only advice is don't ever be afraid to say if you want help. Don't let pride stand in your way, you're only human and you're too good a guy for the company to lose.'

Brad nodded. It was sound advice from the man he respected more than any other on earth.

McNelly lay back for a few moments, gathering his thoughts. Then he said, 'I'm told there's a guy over in Kell County called Earl Solomon. It's been reported that he's taken over the whole county and styles himself King Solomon — somethin' of an English title, I believe.' McNelly allowed himself an ironic smile. 'Tex Logan, the Sheriff of Vance County, has written to me stating his opinion that there is no law

5

and order in Kell but King Solomon's and that no-one can be persuaded to testify against him. Very well, we shall see. Go there, scout the situation, empty a few saddles if you have to and report back. No heroics, mind. If Solomon's position is as strong as they say it is, this may well be a job at company level.'

There was a tap on the door and the two men paused as the nurse appeared. Her wire-rimmed spectacles gave her a cold, unyielding expression.

'I'm afraid I must ask you to leave now,' she said to Brad in a manner which brooked no argument.

McNelly raised his hand in a feeble salute as Brad withdrew.

'One more thing, Sergeant Saunders,' he said as Brad reached the door. He eyed Brad's soiled range clothes with an air of mild distaste. 'Go see a tailor and get yourself some new clothes.'

'But Cap'n, I don't need any new gear.'

'That's an order,' McNelly said, an amused twinkle in his eye. 'Don't think

I've singled you out for special treatment. I've kitted out all the other guys I brought here with me to San Antonio. I want the men of the Special Company to look like lawmen, not a bunch of drifters. Well now, goodbye, Sergeant Saunders — and good luck.'

★   ★   ★

'Boss?'

Earl Solomon leaned back in his chair and drew smoothly on his Havana cigar as Lee Bannerman entered his office.

Solomon's long wavy blond hair, framing the clean-shaven features of his deceptively boyish-looking face, stood in marked contrast to Bannerman's drooping black moustache and gaunt features marred by the livid scar high on his right cheek. His clothes also clashed with the drab range of his ranch foreman, for underneath his gold-embroidered buckskin jacket, Solomon was wearing a shirt of the finest linen with a knotted silk handkerchief about his neck. A crimson sash was tied in such a way that it did not conceal the pair of ivory-handled silver-plated Colts strapped about his slim waist.

But although he dressed like a king, Solomon liked nothing better than to be called 'boss'; in fact that appellation pleased him better than his sobriquet, for although the appearance of a king might command lip-service from his subjects, as their boss, his men obeyed him without question.

'Grimes is bringin' a herd in tomorrow morning,' he said.

Bannerman pulled a face.

'Whatever else you had in mind, ferget it. The factory needs 'em,' Solomon snapped. 'I want this job given priority.'

Bannerman shrugged, 'You're the boss.'

He felt his guts begin to churn. To disguise his feelings, he took out his Durham sack and crafted a smoke.

Does he know I'm sweet on Abigail?

He recoiled mentally, trying to block out the thought of the appalling consequences if Solomon were to find out.

The silver spurs of Solomon's Spanish leather riding-boots jingled as he rose and strode over to a side-table and poured himself a shot of whiskey.

Bannerman ignored his boss's slight in not offering him a drink. Solomon treated everyone in his employ that way — apart from men like Ed Grimes with whom he maintained an atmosphere of restrained respect. But then Ed — or 'Lucifer' as he had been nicknamed by someone in a moment of black humour — was a gunman, and no-one knew how good a gunman was until he faced him . . .

'As soon as this consignment arrives, I want two dozen head sent through to the factory immediately,' Solomon said.

Bannerman drew heavily on his cigarette and nodded. It was typical that Solomon should refer to a herd of stolen cattle as a 'consignment'. But then, despite his appearance Earl Solomon had the reputation of being an astute businessman. 'You got a problem?' Solomon's tenor voice rose to falsetto as he spoke.

Bannerman felt his hackles rising. 'I don't care for handlin' stolen cattle.'

'I don't give a damn about your scruples, Bannerman,' Solomon retorted. 'You ain't got a right to any. You know what? I've always wanted to know what made you tick ever since the day I took over this place.' He opened a drawer, took out a dodger and held it up, his eyes glistening with triumph. 'See this? I found this a while back tucked away in a drawer in Sheriff Vickery's office.'

Bannerman swallowed hard and stared at the dodger. There was no doubt about it, it showed his clear likeness, his real name and the price on his head. The legend *JOHN H. LASCELLES, WANTED FOR MURDER* burned a hole in his brain.

'It wasn't murder, it was self-defence,' he protested.

'That's not the way the rangers see it,' Solomon said smoothly. 'This dodger says there's a bench-warrant out for your arrest for the murder of Jerry Quinn in Galveston.'

'The rangers weren't there,' Bannerman said bitterly. 'Jerry Quinn was a two-bit gambler. He thought he could take me fer a ride. When I called him out he drew a knife on me. I got this scar to prove it.'

Solomon's eyes narrowed. 'If you were so sure you were right, why didn't you stay put and stand trial?'

'There were no other witnesses except his sidekicks. They would have testified against me. I had no choice but to go on the run.'

'Talk's cheap, Bannerman. Fact is, you've killed a guy. It seems to me you got my partner to employ you under false pretences.'

'I told you, I ain't no murderer . . . '

'Oh yeah? Face it, Bannerman, all

this no packing a gun makes you no better than the next man. I could turn you in and claim this reward any time I like. You may have fooled Ben Corrigan with some hard-luck story but you don't fool me. Consider yourself damn lucky you still got a job.'

Bannerman went cold inside. Memories came flooding back of the day he'd found Kate. Outlaws had attacked the staging-post where she had lived with her parents and she'd been raped and murdered. Something seemed to snap inside him and despite his employer's pleading he'd quit his job as ranch foreman and spent his time on the road searching fruitlessly for the revenge that never came. Drinking and gambling, trying to forget the future that had been so cruelly snatched away. Was that why he'd picked the quarrel with Quinn? It was the first time he'd ever killed a man and its effect had been cathartic. He'd never packed a side-arm from that day on . . .

'It's all over and done with now,' he said.

'That's where you're wrong, Bannerman. The rangers keep careful records of all their wanted men. They call it the Book of Knaves. I'm the law in Kell an' what I say goes.' He replaced the dodger in his drawer and locked it. His face broke into a cherubic smile. 'However, I'm prepared to overlook this as long as you continue to do a good job for me.'

Bannerman felt his guts tighten, but he kept his face immobile and his thoughts to himself.

As he left the ranch-house, he caught sight of a woman moving around inside the living-room and felt sick to the bottom of his soul.

What the hell was he going to do about Abigail?

★ ★ ★

'We can't be far away now, boy,' Brad muttered, giving Blaze a pat on the neck.

13

He was three days out of San Antonio and following a sequence of trails which led west across the Frio and the Nueces through a country covered with dense thickets of prickly-pear cactus — the infamous 'catclaw country' — heading towards the Rio Grande along the borders of which sprawled Kell County. This summer had been drier than usual; there had been no rain for several weeks and the stallion's hooves kicked up little puffs of dust as he cantered easily along. The sun still glowed warm on the backs of both man and horse although it would be set in an hour.

Ahead of him, the trail divided, and as Brad eased Blaze closer, he caught sight of the first of the two crudely-fashioned signboards. *DOLORES*, he read with a nod. That was the county seat of Vance which he knew he was now riding through. So the other fork must lead into Kell ... he glanced across at the other signboard and stared at the crudely-formed lettering burned into the unseasoned wood in disbelief.

THIS IS KING SOLOMON'S ROAD
TAKE THE OTHER

'We'll see about that,' he muttered.

He removed his Mexican rawhide lariat from the saddle and tossed the loop over the sign. He backed Blaze off, taking up the slack smoothly along the cowhorn honda until the rope was taut, sensing the powerful muscles of the stallion's shoulders flexing as he did so.

'Hold it, right there, mister!'

Two men on foot emerged from the thicket of prickly-pear.

'Drop your gunbelt and get down outa your saddle nice an' easy,' one of them said.

Brad assessed the quality of the opposition at a glance. These two guys weren't brasada brush-poppers — such hard-working ranch-hands were easily recognizable by their clothing, ripped to shreds from crashing their horses through the catclaw thickets in their ceaseless quest for the vast numbers of unclaimed steers which populated the wilderness of the south-west. Brad had nothing but unreserved respect for those hard-working men. But the man who gave the orders was a tall muscular guy with a cigarette drooping from lips framed with a killer moustache. He was dressed in a fancy check shirt, a calf-skin vest, fancy tooled levis, and was holding a Sharp's rifle. His companion was a heavily-built Mexican dressed in gold-braided finery but, somewhat incongruously, he was holding a spade in his left hand and a Colt in his right. Both men were holding their weapons in the arrogant manner of those used to being feared and obeyed.

'We could've shot you outa hand,' the tall man said with an arrogant smile, 'but before we do, I guess I'm kinda curious as to why a guy should be fool enough to want to pull down yonder sign . . . '

They were the last words he spoke, for as he released his gunbelt and dropped it to the ground Brad's Peacemaker appeared in his hand in an action he'd long since perfected in anticipation of just such an emergency as this.

A startled look appeared in the tall man's eyes as the Peacemaker spurted a wicked jet of flame and the slug slammed into his chest, knocking him backwards.

Before the Mexican could overcome his surprise, Brad had fired again. The man's left elbow went limp and he dropped his Colt as he staggered and fell under the impact of a slug smashing into his upper arm.

Brad recovered his gunbelt, recalled Blaze who had cantered a short distance further along the trail out of harm's way, and, gun in hand, strode over to the prostrate Mexican.

'Do not kill me, *señor, por favor!*' The man was gasping in agony at the pain from his shattered elbow. Great beads of perspiration rolled down his face.

Brad bent down and picked up each of his opponents' weapons in turn and hurled them discus-fashion into a dense thicket of prickly-pear.

That done, he stood over the Mexican eyeing him bleakly. If he was to mention in his report that he had shot both these men dead, he knew that McNelly would let it pass unremarked for the Ranger captain's philosophy was a simple one — if a man was foolish enough to threaten the life of one of his men, then he forfeited his own.

'Do you work for a man called Solomon?' Brad asked the Mexican.

The man nodded.

As Brad pulled open his vest the man's eyes widened as he recognized the badge that proclaimed his office.

'*Los Diablos Tejanos!*'

'Your name?'

'Rafael Morales.'

'And his?'

'Amos Meek.'

'Fetch your horses,' Brad snapped.

He watched as the Mexican staggered along the trail, his left arm hanging uselessly by his side, until he came to where he and his companion had tethered them.

The Mexican waited with growing apprehension as Brad took one of the animals, draped the corpse across its back and made it secure with rope.

'*Señor* Solomon will make you pay for this, believe me . . . '

'No I don't,' Brad snapped. 'Now mount up.'

'But *señor*, I am hurt . . . '

Brad drew his gun, cocked it, and held it to the Mexican's head.

'I said, mount up,' he said softly.

He watched impassively while the man, blaspheming in agony, made several unsuccessful attempts to mount his horse before finally succeeding.

By now, blood was dripping from the Mexican's arm and he was visibly weakening. Having him die was not the object, so Brad fetched a field-dressing from his saddle-bags and used it to staunch the flow of blood. Then he fastened a tow-rope from the horse carrying the corpse to the saddle of the Mexican's mount and led the animals onto the trail so recently pretentiously marked as Solomon's.

'How far is it to Solomon's place?' he asked.

'Three, maybe four hours. But señor,' the man pleaded, 'night is falling. I might bleed to death . . . '

'Just make sure you don't before you reach Solomon,' Brad told him.

With that, he took off his hat and swiped it across the rump of the Mexican's horse, sending it forward at a canter along King Solomon's Road.

2

Early next morning, Lee Bannerman was standing with one foot on the lower rail of a corral fence, upwind of the acrid tang of burning thornbush from the branding-fire, waiting to inspect the cattle Grimes and three of his brothers had brought in. Of the gang, only Lucifer remained, having sent his brothers packing into Kell — an opportunity they had taken without question, preferring to leave the negotiation of financial reward for their recent foray to their elder brother.

Bannerman's task was to judge the condition of each of the steers, and depending on its age and condition condemn it to either rebranding and an extended life on Earl Solomon's Crown Ranch or be sent to Kell for slaughter and subsequent processing at the uncrowned king's highly profitable hide and tallow factory.

Bannerman viewed the cattle with a jaundiced eye. His recent clash with Solomon had unsettled him. He fished out his Durham sack and fashioned a smoke reflectively, so abstracted in fact that he failed to see the hands were waiting on him.

'You ready, boss?' the iron-man called.

'OK, prod 'em in,' Bannerman said, bringing his mind to the job in hand.

'Sure thing.' It was Joel, Grimes' kid brother, who replied. There was a mocking look on his thin-faced features as he set about his task.

'How's he doin'?' Grimes asked Bannerman.

As the big outlaw wiped spittle from his blubbery lips with the back of his hand Bannerman noticed he'd lost the first two fingers on his right hand. It was rumoured he'd lost them in a gunfight. It should have meant the end of the career of any normal right-hander, but Grimes had practised assiduously with his Navy Colt packed for a cross-draw with the left hand until he was satisfied he was just as fast with that as he'd been with his mutilated right.

The outlaw ejected a stream of tobacco-juice into the corral. Dressed in a loud check shirt, fancy vest and levis, he was a thick-set man; his lank black hair brushed shoulders as powerful as an ape's.

Bannerman blew out a cloud of smoke reflectively. Grimes had appeared on the scene just over a year ago with the rebellious youngster in tow.

'This is Joel. He's my kid brother,' he'd told him. 'He's fourteen. He's been living with his stepmother in Jim Wells County. She's died an' I reckon he needs an eye keepin' on him. He's too young to ride with me and his brothers. I guess it won't do him any harm to learn about cattle.'

In between times Bannerman had done his best, but the kid was hard to take — he'd too much of his brothers' wildness in him to settle. The only guy he ever paid heed to was his eldest brother.

'Bit skittish still, is he?' Grimes said with the nearest version he could manage of a tolerant half-smile.

Bannerman gave a non-committal shrug and turned his attention to the job in hand.

This bunch of cattle had been taken by extortion, he was certain of that. The iron-man had his straight bar glowing red and poised ready to cancel the old brand, and Solomon's Crown iron handy to rebrand beneath it. Grimes and his three brothers had long since ceased to bother altering brands with a running-iron. Why should they resort to subterfuge when the cattle could be so easily obtained by intimidation and when there was no-one to prevent it?

'You make damn sure I get a good price, Bannerman,' Grimes growled as the ranch-hands prodded the first beast into the corral and grounded it.

The stink of burning hide filled the

air as the iron-man did his job. As Bannerman leaned forward to inspect the next steer, he felt the devil of resentment flare inside him.

'Whoa there. Hold that one down,' he called out.

It took the united efforts of Joel and another of the younger hands to floor the recalcitrant steer amidst the chaffing of the older hands.

'What's up with you? It's only a calf. Solomon'll wanna keep it,' Grimes demanded as Bannerman ducked low and slipped through the fence to approach the bawling animal.

Bannerman ignored him and bent down to inspect the brand. It hadn't been burned deep enough and was partially obscured by hair.

'Gimme the clippers,' he rapped to the iron-man.

Taking them, Bannerman clipped the hair neatly away to reveal the brand.

'It's the Roman Four,' he said bleakly as he rose to his feet.

'So what?' Grimes growled. 'Look, I

ain't got time to waste. Let's get on with it.'

'The Roman Four is Tex Young's brand,' Bannerman said, conscious of the eyes of the crew watching him.

'So what?'

'Tex has been sick. His wife's havin' trouble enough holdin' his ranch together. If she loses the breeding-stock they're finishd.'

'What do you want me to do? Take 'em back?' Grimes jeered. 'I offered her a fair price and she accepted.'

'I'll bet she did.'

'So what's it to you?'

Bannerman rose to his feet, ice-cold inside.

'You're a bastard, Grimes. A lousy rotten thieving bastard. That's the only decent thing that can be said about you.'

As the outlaw eased his bulk from the fence, the atmosphere in the corral grew tense. Solomon's crew froze to a tableau, their faces grimy in the billows of smoke swirling from the branding-fire.

Bannerman, who had never packed a side-arm since that fateful day in Galveston, faced Grimes fully conscious of the fact that he was physically outmatched as well.

What the hell! he thought. *I'm through with bein' pushed around.*

The first blow came without warning. A vicious, swiping, haymaking right-hander smashing him full in the mouth, crushing his lips to bloody pulp against his teeth, toppling him backwards. He coughed and spat a gobbet of blood. It felt like he'd been clubbed with a fourteen-pound hammer. Only the corral fence prevented him from falling down. Dazed, he clawed his way back to his feet, fighting to clear his vision through the misty-grey veil that had been drawn over it. He passed his hand across his mouth, drawing another spurt of blood from his cut lower lip.

'Go on, smash him, Lucifer!' Joe shouted, dancing up and down in a frenzy of excitement.

Sheer perversity made Bannerman

put his head down and drive forward in a primeval urge to redeem himself. He landed a left and right, raising two satisfying grunts of agony from his opponent as his fists struck into Grimes' slab-muscled torso, just underneath the heart. But Grimes reacted with a flurry of solid punches to the head and body, his arms driving as relentlessly as locomotive piston-rods. As Bannerman rocked back on his heels, the big outlaw laughed triumphantly and braced himself for one final blow.

But Bannerman wasn't beaten yet. He stepped backwards, deliberately riding the blow, drawing Grimes onto a right-hand uppercut that caught him full on the chin. For a brief moment, the outlaw's eyeballs rolled skywards. As he sank onto one knee, his hand moved towards his gun . . . 'Stop it!' a female voice shouted. 'You men stop fighting this minute!'

Grimes, his hand poised over his holster like a rattlesnake before a strike, turned to face the slightly-built woman who came rushing towards him in a flurry of skirts. He backed away as she brushed past him and bent down over Bannerman who had sunk to his knees holding both hands to his mangled, bloodied face.

'What do you men think you are about? You're fighting like a pair of schoolboys.'

Grimes backed off while the woman helped Bannerman to his feet. She eyed the Crown ranch-hands with scorn.

'So you all think it's OK to stand there and do nothing while this man fights with your foreman? Wasn't there one of you man enough to try to stop it?'

There was a great deal of shuffling of feet as the men quailed under the lash of her tongue.

'It ain't our quarrel, Mrs Solomon,' a hand said.

'Bannerman asked for all he got,' Joel said insolently.

Abigail Solomon rounded on him,

her dark eyes blazing with anger.

'Mr Bannerman to you,' she said. 'Must I listen to the words of a child?'

'I ain't no child,' Joel objected peevishly.

'Then talk like a man, *hombre*,' Abigail spat back.

'Now see here, Mrs Solomon . . . ' Grimes began.

'What the hell is goin' on?'

Everyone turned round at the sound of Earl Solomon's high-pitched imperious voice. He strode towards them, his silver spurs jingling. He sized up the situation at a glance.

'Take Bannerman up to the house,' he ordered two of the gawping ranchhands. 'Abigail, go with him and clean him up.' He turned to Grimes. 'Jordan's arrived. Come with me to the office. I want we should talk business.'

Grimes bent down to retrieve his hat. 'What about my cattle?' he grumbled.

'They'll keep,' Solomon snapped over his shoulder as he strode back towards the house.

Once inside his office, Solomon lit a fresh cigar and resumed his seat behind his desk.

'Sorry 'bout that, Jordan,' he said. 'I guess we can get on now Ed's here.'

Jordan Tute nodded. He was a tall, stringy man with a head so devoid of hair and flesh it resembled a skull, out of which two eyes peered as unblinking as an owl's. He was dressed in nondescript range-clothes and packed a pair of Smith and Wessons.

The two outlaws exchanged curt nods.

'What was all that about?' Solomon demanded of Grimes.

The big outlaw fashioned a smoke clumsily in his blood-smeared fingers.

'Bannerman's tryin' to make out I'd robbed a guy who's hit hard times,' he said in his slow way. 'I guess I took exception to that. I bought that herd fair an' square.'

Solomon guffawed. Tute's thin lips parted in a mirthless, gap-toothed smile.

'Listen, Ed, take no notice of Bannerman. He's a loser.'

'If it wasn't for your wife interferin' I'd have finished him,' Grimes growled, exhaling a cloud of smoke. 'I never could figure out a guy who don't pack a gun.'

'Lucky fer you you didn't,' Solomon said smoothly.

The two men's eyes met, each weighing the other up. Solomon won the wordless confrontation and Grimes broke the deadlock first.

'You promised to cut me an' the boys in on the profits,' he said. He screwed his beetle-black eyebrows together. 'Just like you done Jordan here. I'm doin' OK, aren't I?'

Solomon went over to the table, poured three shots of whiskey and passed them round.

'Sure, sure. There's a consignment leaving fer Galveston tomorrow. Ain't that so, Jordan?'

The outlaw nodded.

Solomon turned back to Grimes.

'What's eatin' you, Ed? Why, without me, you an' your brothers would be just another bunch of no-hopers tryin' to keep body and soul together — an' don't you ever forget it.'

Grimes' eyes narrowed as smoke trickled gently out of his mouth and nostrils. He acknowledged the truth of what Solomon was saying with a grudging nod.

'But we done all you asked,' he said harshly. 'Me and my boys bring in enough cattle to keep that factory going. We deserve a spread of our own — just like Jordan's.'

'Sure you do. But as I just been saying to Jordan, we gotta be careful we don't squeeze the lemon dry.'

Grimes stared at Solomon, clearly mystified. 'What's lemons got to do with it?'

Solomon and Tute eyed him with amused contempt.

'Listen, Ed, between us we got Kell squeezed 'til the pips squeak. We gotta move further out — expand. Don't you agree, Jordan?'

Tute gave an almost imperceptible nod.

'OK, you're the boss,' Grimes said with a shrug.

'I am — an' don't you ever forget it!' Solomon's clear tenor voice rose almost to falsetto as he spoke. 'I'm runnin' this show an' I got plenty of guys who'll back me if you or anyone steps outa line.'

'OK,' Grimes replied. 'What you say goes. There ain't no law here in Kell. There ain't a single ranch or business fer a hundred miles that don't pay you in money or cattle to protect them . . . '

'You're forgettin' about Dolores,' Solomon said softly.

'Dolores? Why, that's in Vance County.'

'So it is,' Solomon agreed.

'Now wait a minute,' Grimes said. 'You just said you got Kell all stitched up. Why stretch yourself? Tex Logan is the law in Vance County an' he's made it plain he ain't lookin' fer trouble. Why not leave well alone?'

Solomon rose and walked over to the

window. As he did so, Peach, a mulatto servant-girl, walked past carrying a pitcher of water. Solomon saw her and smiled.

'I don't believe I'm hearin' you, Ed,' he said, dragging his mind back to business in hand. 'You keep tellin' me you're havin' to travel further and further afield to get cattle. Now I reckon that at the rate you're working, the day will come when the ranchers in this county will have nothin' left . . . '

'But what about Logan?'

'OK, I'll allow he used to be a good lawman. Time was when I wouldn't have even thought of taking him on. But he's gettin' long in the tooth and he ain't lookin' fer trouble. A slack lawman makes a town a soft touch, didn't we prove that here in Kell? Now I figure once I've got control over Dolores, I got control over Vance County; then there'll be cattle aplenty to supply the factory, maybe even build another.'

As Solomon paused, a fervent, almost mystical look appeared in his eyes.

'Once we got Vance in control, we keep movin'. I'm gonna be the richest man in the whole of the south-west. Ain't that right, Jordan?'

Tute nodded.

Grimes looked sceptical. 'Logan may be past it, but what about the rangers?'

'What about 'em? McNelly's a dyin' man. Gone to San Antonio to meet his Maker, so they say. Well, it's good riddance. I've heard that his way of doin' things is none too popular with the pot-bellies back in Austin. I figure that once he's dead, the authorities there will disband his company. Anyways, there ain't room for two kings around here, so don't you worry none about rangers.'

'So what do you want me and the boys to do?'

'Get busy in Vance,' Solomon snapped. 'Jordan's boys have already made a start. Now I want the pair of you to put the screws on. Put the fear of God into 'em.' His face broke out into an engaging smile. 'It's gonna work, Ed, believe me. Just like it's done here in Kell.'

'It could be we're takin' somethin' on,' Grimes muttered. His bloodstained hand roughed against the stubble on his cheek reflectively as he spoke.

'I'll be the judge of that,' Solomon said. 'Now here's a promise. Once we've taken Vance I'll cut you into a nice little spread, just like Jordan. Is that a deal?'

'OK, you're the boss,' Grimes muttered as he headed for the door.

When the door closed behind him, Solomon's knuckles clenched white as the sensation of power coursed through his veins, lifting him higher than two shots of whiskey ever could.

'It's gonna work, Jordan, it really is,' he said, slapping the tall outlaw across the shoulder.

Tute's lips curled back over his yellow teeth in a wolfish grin.

'You reckon?'

'Sure I do. Once we've taken Vance we'll recruit more men, an' with your boys and Ed's we'll be a match for anyone. Stick with me, Jordan, I'm gonna be the king of south-west Texas.'

'Sure boss, you can rely on me.'

A knock on the door galvanized Solomon. His eyes lit up with pleasure. No doubt it would be Peach . . . but when he opened it, to his disgust he found Joel Grimes standing outside.

'What do you want?' Solomon snapped.

'I guess there's somethin' you oughta know,' the boy said excitedly. 'A Mex called Rafael Morales has just ridden in. He's badly shot up.'

Solomon turned to Tute. 'Morales? He's one of your men, ain't he?'

Tute nodded.

'Run into trouble, did he?' Solomon asked Joel.

'Can't tell you more, Mr Solomon. But he's sure had a tough time. But that ain't all. He's brought a horse in totin' another guy — Amos Meek — he's been shot dead . . . '

3

Brad rose at dawn and after a frugal breakfast of tinned beans and coffee he set out to follow the forbidden trail into Kell County. His plan was simple; once the Mexican reached Solomon and told his story, Solomon would have to do something — the question was, what? The nature of the man's reaction would determine how formidable he really was. The annals of the rangers were full of stories of bravos who melted away as soon as the heat was on. But Brad reckoned this guy Solomon was made of sterner stuff. However, time would tell . . .

As he cantered along, from time to time his keen eyes caught the occasional spatters of blood which marked the wounded man's passage. Brad had dismissed the man's claim he was dying with the contempt it deserved; during the war he'd seen men survive far worse.

Apart from the odd maverick eyeing him balefully as it lurked in the prickly-pear thickets, and the occasional sighting of javelina, the countryside seemed quiet enough. But suddenly Brad caught a smell in his nostrils which made every westerner in the wilderness sit up and take notice — the smell of burning. He reined Blaze in and surveyed the trail ahead, searching for signs of an old camp-fire, but at first he could see nothing. The stink of burning wood on the warm breeze was faint, but unmistakable. He pushed on a little further along the trail until he reached a rise and paused again. This time he caught sight of a plume of smoke wafting lazily in the heat-haze.

Turning to rummage in his saddle-bag he found his brass-bound spyglass. The windmill was clearly visible, and focusing at the base of the plume of smoke he could clearly see the charred remains of a burned-out building.

Puzzled, he snapped the instrument shut and pondered. There was no Indian trouble in these parts. The smoking ruin lay off the trail about a mile or so to the north-west towards the county line. It could even be in Vance. Best he ride directly over to investigate.

Without hesitating, he dismounted and pulled on a pair of bull-hide leggings. He'd long since changed out of the fancy new gear McNelly had kitted him out with in favour of his well-worn shirt, vest and pants. Then he remounted and moved Blaze off the trail into the prickly-pear thicket, allowing the massive-chested stallion to find its way while he maintained a general line in the direction of the smouldering building. The leggings protected him from the catclaw.

An hour later, he emerged out of an arroyo into more open country a quarter of a mile from the remains of what once had been a small ranch-house close to which there was a stand of hackberry trees and a field of alfalfa.

As he approached closer, several unbroken mustangs whickered and milled around in a small corral. The owner probably made his living breaking-in and selling animals roaming the surrounding country.

Brad dismounted and led Blaze across to the water-trough beside the windmill and allowed the stallion to drink his fill. As Brad filled his hat to slake his own thirst he was aware of the mill turning overhead with an eerie creaking noise — the sucker-rods and gears needed a regular dousing with oil.

Refreshed, he walked across to what was left of the ranch-house. The flames had died down, but the smouldering ruin was still sending up wisps of evil-smelling smoke.

Where were the occupants?

He combed the surrounding area thoroughly searching for sign. As he worked, a picture began to build up in his mind — one that he liked less and less as time went on. Finally, he knew what he had to do . . .

The ground was still hot inside what was left of the building — the ferocity of the blaze had razed the wooden structure to the ground. As he stepped gingerly inside he saw with a sinking heart what he feared most. The material of a woman's dress was fluttering in the warm breeze . . .

He moved further inside, sweat pouring off him in the radiant heat from the embers. Coming closer he saw not one, but two half-charred bodies lying side by side close by the doorway.

A man and his wife?

It was too hot to go closer so Brad pulled out and returned to Blaze to fetch his lariat.

When he came back to the house he set about the grisly task of recovering the bodies with the aid of the rope. But before he could accord them a decent burial, he was faced with the grim task of identification.

In order to inspect them closely he was compelled to tie his bandanna tightly round his mouth and nose to avoid the nauseating smell of roasted flesh.

As he expected, identification was impossible but his surmise that they were man and wife was borne out by the fact that the woman was wearing a wedding-ring.

Suddenly his mouth tightened. As he turned each corpse over he detected a bullet-hole in their backs. He straightened up slowly, his face set hard. It was clear that the couple had been murdered and an attempt made to incinerate their bodies in the flames.

Behind him, Blaze whickered. As Brad whirled round, the Peacemaker appeared in his hand with the precision of a well-oiled machine. Only his iron self-disicpline prevented him from emptying the weapon at the figure approaching him through the haze of smoke . . .

★ ★ ★

Bannerman's spinning head came to a slow, painful stop, allowing his eyes to come gradually back into focus. Cool fingers smoothed his forehead and warm water dribbled down his cheek, splashing onto his bare chest.

'This water isn't hot enough. See to it, Peach.' Abigail's gentle voice seemed to echo bell-like in his increasing level of consciousness.

'But I only just brought it,' the girl objected.

Even in his half-dazed condition. Bannerman detected the note of protest in the servant's voice.

'Do it!'

Peach recoiled at the venom in her mistress's tone and hastened to do as she was told.

'I don't know what's got into that girl just lately,' Abigail said softly as she continued to dab the blood from Bannerman's face.

His eyes focused on the dark beauty of Abigail's face, marred only by the deep furrows of concern on her forehead. The richly-scented perfume of her presence was overwhelming. Solomon must be crazy to treat a woman like her so badly.

'Abigail,' he muttered, taking her hand in his.

She withdrew her hand and stared at him. 'Why, what are you thinking of, Mr Bannerman?'

Embarrassed, Bannerman turned his face away and reached for his shirt. He tensed involuntarily as Abigail wiped the water from his back with a heart-stopping caress.

Her eyes softened as she touched the scar on his cheek. 'Take care of yourself, *caballero*,' she whispered. 'Don't soil your hands on men like Grimes.'

Bannerman slipped on the clean shirt she handed to him. Outside, the cattle Grimes had brought were lowing impatiently.

'He's robbin' people blind of their cattle,' he muttered, half to himself. 'Payin' 'em peanuts for 'em.'

Abigail buttoned the front of his shirt for him, her slim fingers moving dextrously.

'Do you think I don't know what's going on?' she demanded. 'I've got eyes and ears.' Her voice dropped a tone. 'I'll tell you somethin', Mr Bannerman; Earl is not half the man Ben was.'

Bannerman nodded bleakly, relieved that at last Abigail was expressing her misgivings openly. She was referring, of course, to her first husband, Ben Corrigan. He and Earl Solomon had been business partners; Ben had looked after the ranch, Earl the hide and tallow factory. One day Bannerman had found Ben's body in the barn. He had been strangled to death with his bandanna. Sheriff Vickery had investigated diligently but his killer had never been found. Solomon's subsequent marriage to Abigail six months later had given him complete control of the business.

Were the two events connected? Bannerman had no proof, but he'd always had a gut feeling that Solomon had either murdered his business partner himself or paid one of his henchmen to do it.

Bannerman had respected Ben Corrigan, for the rancher had taken him on without asking questions when his fortunes were at a low ebb and had given him the chance to earn an honest living.

He put his hand on Abigail's arm, but as she pushed him gently away, there was a look of longing in her eyes.

'No, Lee!' she whispered in a husky voice.

As she did so, the door opened and Peach reappeared holding a pail of hot water. Bannerman noticed with dismay the flash of perception in the girl's eyes — *she knew there was something between them!*

He bit his lower lip, drawing the bitter taste of blood from the cut. Did Abigail know it was common knowledge that her husband took Peach whenever he felt like it? If she did, she gave no sign of it.

'You are too late, now,' Abigail said with a dismissive wave of her slender hand. 'Use it to wash Mr Bannerman's shirt.'

The girl eyed Abigail with a sullen expression which Bannerman for a moment thought would explode into open revolt before she picked up the bloodstained shirt, dropped it into the pail of water, turned and left them.

'These servants get worse,' Abigail said with a sigh when Peach had gone.

Even as the door closed it burst open again and Joel stuck his head round it, an insolent smirk on his face

'Mrs Solomon, there's a guy outside. He's hurt real bad.' He looked cheekily at Bannerman. 'Mr Solomon is askin' iffen you're ready to deal with them steers. Lu's waitin' on you.'

'Don't you ever knock?' Bannerman said exasperatedly to Joel as they left the house.

'Why should I?'

'Now listen, boy!' Bannerman exploded, grabbing him by the collar.

Joel wrested himself free and stared defiantly back at him. 'But for Mrs Solomon, Lu would've finished you just now. Come to think of it, you never did say why you don't pack a gun.'

'Why you cheeky young polecat!'

As Bannerman's fists balled Joel stood off holding his fists in the attitude of a prizefighter.

'Come on then!' he taunted.

Bannerman regained control of himself with an effort. Knocking the hell out of Grimes' kid brother would do nothing to enhance his standing with the hands. He left the kid and strode acoss to the corral where Solomon was still chewing the fat with Grimes and Tute.

'You tellin' me this guy outdrew Amos Meek?' Solomon was saying incredulously.

'Rafael reckons they had the drop on him,' Tute said.

'I don't believe it,' Solomon replied.

'Best I send some of the boys to check it out,' Tute drawled, hitching up his gunbelt. He was plainly rattled; his usually gaunt features were as sepulchral as a recently interred corpse.

'You do that, Jordan,' Solomon said approvingly. 'Rafael reckons the guy's a ranger. Iffen he is, the sooner we deal with him the better.'

A ranger!

Bannerman felt his guts lurch. What the hell was a ranger doing in Kell County? Surely they weren't still looking for him?

He watched as two hands carried Meek's body away for burial on a crude stretcher fashioned from fence-poles. Amos Meek had a reputation for being handy with a gun, yet a single ranger on whom he'd had the drop had killed him and badly wounded his companion . . .

Tute was now fully in control of himself, his eyes cold and expressionless once more. He acknowledged Bannerman with a nod and walked back to the ranch-house with Solomon.

With reluctance Bannerman applied

himself to the task of sorting the herd of stolen cattle. Fortunately, Grimes soon got bored and kept his distance. Only when he was good and ready did Bannerman make out a chit and gave it to him to take to Solomon's clerk for payment. He watched the outlaw's departure with a mixture of suppressed anger and profound relief.

'Lofty's takin' a wagon into town for supplies,' Joel said to Bannerman later when Grimes had gone. 'Can I go along and give him a hand?'

'Sure,' Bannerman sad wearily, for his busted mouth was hurting like hell. The kid's cocky attitude irritated him beyond endurance. 'Go with him and stay outa my sight fer a while.'

It was plain to Bannerman that the youngster wanted to head into town where he knew he would meet up with his brothers.

'OK — boss,' Joel said with a smirk.

★ ★ ★

'Hold it right there!' Brad ordered.

But even as he spoke, the figure staggered and then collapsed like a rag doll.

Brad holstered his weapon and covered the intervening ground with giant strides. The body was lying close to Blaze. The big stallion was edgy, but in the way of all trained horses he kept clear of the inert body.

As he knelt down Brad saw it was a youth. He lifted him up in one easy movement and carried him away from the horror of the house into the meagre shade afforded by a hackberry tree. Then he fetched his canteen and gave him water.

Hell's teeth, what am I gonna do? he thought.

The youth was fair-haired, slightly built. His big round eyes, blue as the sky, stared at Brad, full of fear and suspicion.

'Don't be afraid, boy,' Brad said, displaying his badge. 'I'm a Texas Ranger. What's your name?'

When the youth didn't answer, he tried again.

'Listen, son, I'm a lawman. I ain't here to harm you.'

Slowly, the fear ebbed away from the boy's eyes.

'I'm Jamie McDonald,' he whispered.

'Are you hurt, Jamie?' Brad asked after he'd given him another sip of water.

'I guess it's my ankle.'

He cried out as Brad tried to remove his riding-boot. Brad took out his Bowie knife and sliced through the leather. Once the boot was removed it revealed a nasty swelling on the outside of the joint but he could not be sure if it was broken. His lips tightened with exasperation; there was so little he could do. He went over to Blaze, fetched a bandage from his medical kit and bound it round the ankle as tightly as was comfortable.

'Did you see what happened here?' he asked casually as he worked.

The lad's face twitched for a moment

and then suddenly the words came gushing out like a torrent of water through an arroyo after heavy rain.

'I was ridin' one of the mustangs pa had just broken in when I saw the fire. I headed for home but the hoss stumbled and threw me. I must have hit my head and passed out. When I came to I found I'd hurt my ankle real bad. The hoss had run off so I had to get back as best I could. It took me ages. By the time I arrived the house had been burned down.'

'And your ma and pa?'

'I guess you've seen for yourself,' the boy said bitterly.

'You any idea who did this?'

The boy shook his head.

'Was there two of 'em?'

The boy stared at Brad. 'How did you know that?'

'I read the sign.'

Brad sat back and fished for his Durham sack in the breast pocket of his vest.

'Jamie, this is important. Did you get

a look at these two guys?'

'Yeah, they were gettin' ready to leave as I arrived. I was scared so I hid up until they'd gone, not realizing what they'd done to ma and pa.'

'Can you describe, 'em?'

'One was a tall, rangy guy; the other was a big fat Mex.'

Brad cursed inwardly. If he'd known this last night he would have sent two corpses back to Solomon, not one.

'I guess they tried to rob your pa and he wouldn't pay up,' he observed.

The youth shot him a scornful look. 'What do you think? Pa was the stubbornest guy this side of the Rio Grande. He was brave, too. He fought with Stonewall in the Shenandoah Valley. He never spoke much about it, but he once told me that after all he'd seen in the war, he was frightened of no man. Were you in the war, mister?'

Brad nodded. He knew how the boy's father felt. Given the choice after Jeb Stuart, the one man he'd have chosen to serve with was the legendary

Stonewall Jackson.

Brad looked about him. 'Say, Jamie, did you spend the night alone out here?'

The youth nodded. 'Just saw a coupla javelinas but they don't scare me none.'

Brad shook his head in wonderment. The raw courage of this taciturn frontier-lad impressed him. The future of Texas would be in safe hands if only men like Solomon could be brought to book.

Jamie regarded him coolly. 'So what you gonna do now, mister ranger-man?'

Brad said nothing. The kid was entitled to give vent to his bitterness and anger. He would never forget the day he found his own father dead with an arrow between his shoulder-blades. He rose and walked over to Blaze.

'Hey, mister, you ain't gonna leave me, are you?' The note in Jamie's voice changed from contempt to anxiety.

'What do you take me for?' Brad replied. 'Jamie, I have to tell you that I guess you won't be gettin' no more

57

trouble from those two guys. I came up with 'em late yesterday by the fork in the trail. The tall guy is dead an' the Mex is badly wounded.'

Jamie stared at him in astonishment. Suddenly his eyes narrowed.

'Now you ain't just sayin' that, are you, mister?'

'Jamie, when the day comes I don't tell the truth about a thing like that, I'll throw in my badge. Now I understand those guys were working fer a man called Solomon . . . '

'King Solomon!' Jamie exclaimed. 'I heard pa say he was a real bad guy who wanted to boss everybody around.'

Brad nodded. 'I sent the Mex back to Kell with the other guy's body.'

The kid's eyes widened. 'You did?'

Brad nodded. 'By now I guess Solomon's got the message a Texas Ranger is around.'

'When he finds out what's happened he's gonna come lookin' fer you. We'd best move outa here,' Jamie said in alarm.

'Is there someplace I can take you?'

'Pa's cousin keeps a store in Dolores.'

'How far is it?'

'It's about half a day's ride. If you could get me there maybe the doc will fix my ankle. Problem is I ain't got a broken-in hoss.'

'That ain't no problem, Blaze can take two up.'

'Sure he can,' the lad said admiringly. He patted Blaze on the muzzle. 'Say, mister, what a beaut! He must weigh all of a thousand pounds.'

'OK,' Brad said. 'We'll leave after I've buried your ma and pa.'

He left the boy to rest while he set about his melancholy task with the aid of a spade, the shaft of which had been burned so badly he had need to improvise another from the branch of a tree. It was hard work, and when he'd finished he made a rough cross and placed it over the grave. That done, he paused. Should he fetch the boy and show him what he'd done? Maybe he wouldn't be up to it . . .

59

'Would you say a prayer?' Jamie asked quietly. Brad had been so busy he was unaware the boy was standing watching him.

Hat in hand, he did as the boy requested.

'OK if we go now?' Jamie asked when he'd finished.

'Sure,' he said. The boy's lack of tangible grief seemed unnatural. Glancing upwards, his keen eyes caught a quail rising in the sky.

Jamie's eyes followed Brad's. 'I guess it won't be long before we got company. D'you reckon it'll be Solomon's men?' he asked anxiously.

'Only one way to find out,' Brad replied.

When they reached Blaze, Brad made to help the lad into the saddle but he limped past him, heading towards the corral.

'Hey, Jamie, we'd best get movin',' Brad called out urgently.

Jamie ignored him as he lifted the bar to the corral. He scarcely had time to stand aside as the mustangs erupted from their prison in a flurry of hooves and charged into catclaw.

'I couldn't leave 'em,' Jamie said apologetically as Brad led Blaze towards him. 'Not without food an' water. Pa would never have forgiven me.'

When kids like this grow into men, guys like Solomon had best look out! Brad thought grimly as he helped him up into the saddle.

He urged Blaze into the catclaw and after about an hour of riding drew to a halt on a barren rocky outcrop in the centre of more open country.

He took out the spyglass and scanned the horizon.

'Are they followin' us?' Jamie enquired.

Brad snapped the instrument shut.

'Reckon so.'

Jamie watched him as he dismounted and made to lift him down.

'Shouldn't we get the hell outa here, mister?' he asked anxiously.

'It ain't my job to run,' Brad replied.

Jamie looked about him and shivered

as he caught sight of a cloud of dust on the skyline.

'Hey, mister, what are you gonna do?' he demanded as Brad withdrew his Winchester from its scabbard and checked the loads.

'There's cover aplenty in these rocks,' Brad said. 'Get down, boy, and stay down. Don't even think of raising your head.'

Pale with fear, the lad did as he was told. Brad lay Blaze down alongside him, crafted a smoke and then forted himself in the rocks between them and the oncoming riders.

There were four of them, spread out, approaching at a canter. Sitting ducks — just like the Union cavalry in the early days of the war.

As he cradled the Winchester against his cheek he recalled McNelly's words: 'Empty a few saddles if you have to.'

From where he lay in the sun-baked rocks he watched patiently as the riders drew closer . . . and closer.

They disappeared temporarily from

view as they plunged deep into a draw. He could hear their shouts and curses as they twisted this way and that in the catclaw thickets, first losing his trail, now finding it.

Brad stubbed his cigarette out as the first rider emerged from the draw.

'He went this way, boys,' the guy shouted.

Brad waited until all four joined up. They were a typical bunch of the brasada hardcases McNelly had sworn to eliminate like vermin. As they moved forward, he revealed his presence and confronted them, kneeling amongst the rocks, the Winchester tucked into his shoulder.

'OK, boys, hold it right there,' he ordered.

The look of incredulity on the men's unshaven faces would have been amusing had the situation not been so fraught with danger.

Three of them obeyed instinctively, raising their hands, but one man's hand strayed to his holster.

Brad's Winchester barked. The man clapped both hands to his heart and toppled slowly out of his saddle, dead before he hit the ground. The other horses shied and reared as the man's companions fought to control them.

'Anyone else wanna try his luck?' Brad said calmly.

The three other men lifted their hands high and kept them there. They were smart enough to know that a handgun at fifty paces was no match for a marksman with a fully loaded Winchester.

'Now drop your hands one by one and let your gunbelts go,' Brad ordered the men. 'You first,' he said to the man on his right.

One by one, they did as he ordered.

'I guess you must be the ranger who shot Amos Meek,' one of the men muttered.

Brad smiled mirthlessly.

So word had got back to Solomon!

Jamie scrambled to his feet and

limped forward. When he saw the body he turned pale.

'Is he dead?' he asked Brad.

'I gave him his chance to stay alive and he didn't take it,' Brad replied.

Jamie stared at the three men.

Brad passed him the Winchester. 'Jamie, you keep 'em covered while I rope 'em up. You feel up to that?'

Jamie took the weapon and cocked it. 'Sure. Say, are these guys comin' with us?'

'They ain't got no choice,' Brad said cynically.

He removed a lariat from one of the men's horses and cut off three lengths.

Suddenly, seeing his chance, one of the men broke and ran for his horse. Before Brad could draw his Peacemaker, Jamie had fired the Winchester, but the deflection shot at the moving target eluded him and the man leapt onto his horse and crashed headlong into the brush.

'I think I winged him!' the boy exclaimed excitedly.

'One less to deal with,' Brad observed as he began to lash one of the men's hands behind him. 'We shan't see him again. I guess he'll give Solomon a mite more fat to chew on.'

A few minutes later, Brad had completed the task of securing his prisoners astride their horses; then he helped the boy onto the spare horse belonging to the dead rider.

'OK, Jamie,' he said, after he had mounted Blaze. 'Next stop, the jail at Dolores.'

4

It was early afternoon when Lofty and Joel hit town.

'How long do I get?' Joel asked eagerly as they pulled the buckboard up outside the store.

'Waal, I guess I'll be needin' ya to help me load the flour,' the old-timer replied, scratching his nose.

Joel shielded his eyes against the glare of the sun as he gazed appealingly at Lofty.

'Aw naw, you don't need me fer that, do you?' he wheedled. 'Surely the storeman'll give you a lift?'

Lofty smiled indulgently. He ejected a stream of tobacco-juice at a fly which had just settled on the hitching-post. 'Mr Bannerman gave me strict instructions I was to keep an eye on you.'

'Aw c'mon, Lofty . . . '

'Waal, I suppose I could let you off

the hook fer an hour. But no going in them there saloons, mind — I guess you ain't old enough fer drinkin', gamblin' an' women. Your brother wouldn't like it, either.'

'Aw, Lofty, stop treatin' me like I was a kid.'

Lofty's face broke into a grin, showing a set of teeth that would have done credit to the horse he was tethering.

'Waal, I guess you can't get into too much bother this side o' sundown. But don't be late, otherwise you're on Shanks' pony.'

'Thanks, Lofty,' Joel said as he darted off along the sidewalk.

But in truth, Kell City, as it was somewhat pretentiously called on the map of Texas, had very little to offer other than two rows of clapboard houses, a handful of corrugated iron-walled shops and saloons, a couple of whorehouses and a cluster of Mexican *jacals* which housed the workers at the evil-smelling hide and tallow factory.

Numerous pigs, interspersed with packs of dogs, roamed the rutted streets freely and, together with swarms of flies, nourished on the offal from the factory, contributed to an ambience which hardly resembled a busy metropolis although the place was the county seat. This latter status was demeaned sharply by the empty sheriff's office and the deserted shell of the partially burned-out courthouse which had once occupied pride of place. It was said that King Solomon had deemed that the retention of a comprehensive set of court records was unnecessary in view of the permanent absence of the judge and the sheriff.

But the ambience was not what young Joel was looking for. He had cadged the lift into this seedy border-town for one purpose only. A quick tour of the deserted saloons revealed no sign of his brother. He paused outside a place which seemed somewhat different. The sign said, 'Micah's Place'.

He coughed as he entered the smoke-filled atmosphere and headed for the bar. The place was crowded although it was still only early afternoon.

'I'll have a beer, please,' he said to the shirt-sleeved barkeep.

'See here, we don't serve no boys,' the barkeep said with a gap-toothed grin.

Joel bridled at the rebuff. 'Surely I can drink a beer if I want to.'

The barkeep roared with laughter. He wiped hands the size of dinner-plates on his soiled white apron. 'Say, fellas, here's a sassy boy who says he got the right to drink with the men!'

'I guess I've come to speak with Lucifer Grimes,' Joel said, his narrow chest swelling with importance. 'He's my brother.'

'Hey, Ed, will you listen to this, this boy here's claimin' kinship,' the barman called out.

The bar fell quiet as Grimes turned slowly round and glared at Joel.

'What the hell are you doin' in here? I thought I told you to stay outa town.'

'I hitched a ride in, Lu. I didn't get a chance to talk to you at the ranch. I guess I thought I'd stop by and see the boys.'

'You shouldn't be in here,' Grimes growled. 'You're too young.'

'Say, that was some whuppin' you gave Bannerman this mornin',' Joel enthused, completely unaware of his brother's meaning.

'I guess he had it comin' to him.'

'You bet!' Joel said enthusiastically.

His eldest brother looked even more puzzled.

'What's wit' you, boy? You sound pleased as a dog with two tails.'

'I'm pig sick of Bannerman treatin' me as though I was still a kid. I wish you'd finished him. Didn't you ever wonder why he don't pack a gun? Well, I reckon he's yellow right through to the core. Did you know he's sweet on the boss's wife?'

Grimes stared at him. 'You what?'

71

'Aw, it's no big deal, I guess.'

Grimes guffawed. 'No big deal? Hey, Bill!' he called over to the bartender. 'Give my kid brother a beer.'

Joel collected his glass of beer from the bar and followed the bulky figure of his brother as he threaded his way through the blue haze of smoke towards the table where his other brothers, Zeke and the twins Jud and Curt, were sat playing cards at a green baize-covered table along with another man.

'Hey, señor, you come alonga me. I make your first time ver' nice.' A garishly painted Mexican honkytonk, her hands on her ample hips, thrust her breasts brazenly against him as he brushed past her.

Grimes silenced her with an angry glance. As the outlaw drew closer to the card table, his face took on a puzzled expression.

'So where's Frank?' he demanded.

The twins laid their cards down on the table and regarded their brother as solemnly as high priests interrupted at a sacred rite. They were dressed in suits cut from the same loud check cloth. Their jet-black hair was neatly trimmed and they were clean-shaven except for their drooping moustaches; they were so alike, it was virtually impossible to tell them apart.

The other man they were playing poker with rose and left on the nod from Grimes.

'Frank's taken sick,' Jud replied ponderously as he acknowledged Joel with a nod.

'Sick?' Grimes repeated incredulously. 'How come? Frank ain't never been sick in his life.'

'He is now,' Curt said with a snigger.

'Understanding dawned slowly across Grimes' rugged features. 'Why d'you mean he's been . . . '

'Fornicatin's the word you're searchin' for,' Jud said with a cynical laugh.

'Fornicatin'? What's that mean?' Joel asked plaintively.

Zeke said nothing, but Jud and Curt hung limp with silent laughter until their eldest brother sat down heavily opposite them and fixed them with a cold stare.

'It ain't funny,' he said harshly. 'I take it Frank can't fork a saddle?'

'You're durned right he can't,' Jud said, wiping the tears of laughter away on his shirt-sleeve. 'But we did warn him, didn't we, Curt?'

Before the twins could dissolve into laughter again, Grimes leaned across the table and grabbed them both by the neck. 'Shut-up,' he said. 'This is serious. We got work to do.'

At this sudden flash of temper, Jud and Curt decided it would be prudent to be serious.

'What's that?' Zeke demanded.

Grimes glanced about him. In the hubbub of the saloon, no-one was paying any attention to them. In making his explanation, he failed to notice the keen interest of young Joel who was still hanging round them, cautiously sipping his beer.

'We're movin' into Vance County.'

'Vance?' Zeke said incredulously as he lit a thin cigar. 'What gives? We never stepped over the county line before.'

'There's always a first time. Pity about Frankie,' Curt said reflectively. 'We're gonna be busy for a while.'

'I figure this is gonna need all of us,' Jud said, scratching his head. 'Frank's handy with a gun.'

'Supposin' we recruit someone,' Curt suggested.

'I don't like takin' on anyone else,' Zeke said. 'We've never needed to before.'

'You're right. We're family. We work as a team,' Jud said. 'We'll just have to manage without him, I guess.'

'I could take Frank's place.'

The outlaws turned to stare at Joel.

'No!' Grimes shouted, so loudly that half the men in the vicinity fell silent and the other half reached for their guns. 'Now get out of here, kid; go back to the ranch.'

'But, Lu . . . '

'No buts; on yer hoss, pronto.'

'Shan't! I wanna stay here and ride with you an' the boys.'

Joel's voice rose a notch as his brother's hand grasped his bandanna and tightened.

'Now see here, boy, you ain't talkin' to that yeller-bellied ranch foreman now. When I say go, you do it or I'll take my belt to your ass. Now get outa here!'

A few moments later a disgruntled Joel was approaching the store.

His jaw sagged open in disbelief.

The buckboard had gone!

'Sorry, son,' the white-haired patriarch who owned the place said in answer to his query as to Lofty's departure. 'The old-timer waited as long as he dared. In the end he reckoned you'd bunked off.'

Joel couldn't believe his ears.

'But it's ten miles back to the ranch!' he protested.

The patriarch tamped baccy into his pipe and lit up. He cast a professional eye over Joel's riding-boots.

'Guess them boots weren't made fer

walkin'. But I could let yuh have a pair of sodbuster's boots on account.'

'Like hell you can!' Joel threw over his shoulder as he stormed out of the store.

★ ★ ★

The day was well advanced when Brad led Jamie and his two prisoners into the sprawling suburb of Mexican *jacals* which preceded Dolores.

The appearance of the little cavalcade of two prisoners accompanied by a young lad and escorted by a tall well-built man sitting astride a magnificent black stallion was sufficient to cause small numbers of interested spectators to gather in speculative groups on the sidewalks.

'Lor sakes, ain't that young Jamie McDonald?'

That hard fact and a host of rumour flew ahead of the cavalcade until it reached the ears of Sheriff Tex Logan. He laid his pen to one side, blotted the report he was writing, and with a sigh rose and walked to the door of his office just as Brad was dismounting outside.

'Why, pa, that's Jamie McDonald!'

It was Cally, Logan's daughter, who confirmed the rumour. She was a big raw-boned girl, dressed in calico, who looked older than her twenty years. She put down a wicker basket full of shopping on her father's desk and when she saw the lad's plight she ran forward to assist him to dismount.

'Why, Jamie, whatever happened to your ankle? Does it hurt bad? Come here, let me help you into Pa's office.'

'Hey, gerroff!' Jamie exclaimed, his face as red as a cock's comb. 'I don't want none of your fussin'.'

'Lordy, lordy, will you hear him!' an onlooker exclaimed. 'Give him another coupla years and he'll be singin' another tune to a pretty gal like that.'

Brad tethered the horses, pleased that someone was prepared to take responsibility for the boy. Then, in front of an audience, he cut the ropes securing the prisoners' ankles under the bellies of the horses and stood aside to allow them to dismount as best they could.

'Al Quater an' Pete Moses!' Logan exclaimed. 'I warned the pair of 'em not to show their ugly snouts here again. Guess you'd better come inside.'

Brad escorted the two men up the steps onto the boardwalk, straight through the office and into the cell Logan opened up for them.

After he'd locked up, Logan opened his desk drawer, dropped the keys inside and faced Brad.

'You some kinda lawman, mister?' he asked bluntly.

'He's a Texas Ranger,' Jamie said in an awed voice. 'Man, you shoulda seen him, he's faster'n a rattlesnake with a gun . . . ouch!' He grimaced with pain as Cally touched his strapped ankle.

'Thought you was a real tough hombre,' the girl grinned. 'That ankle looks in bad shape to me. Look, I saw Doc Ryan goin' into the mortician's office just now. I'll go ask him if he'll come and take a look-see.'

Logan's lined face lit up as Brad drew back his lapel to reveal his badge.

'A Ranger! Am I glad to see one of you boys!' he exclaimed.

He listened in silence while Brad outlined what had happened.

'So they murdered Bill McDonald and his wife,' he muttered when Brad had finished. 'I guess I hoped it would never come to this . . . '

They were interrupted by the arrival of Doc Ryan in his gig. A big, calm man, Ryan did a quick inspection of Jamie's injured ankle.

'Yep, I'm afraid it's broken,' he said laconically, confirming Brad's suspicions. 'I'll have to take him back to my office. I can do the splinting job properly then. I guess you're gonna be hobbling around on crutches for a few weeks, Jamie.'

'I'll go with him,' Cally said, before her father could ask.

'There ain't no need . . . ' Jamie said. Suddenly he screwed his fists into his eyes, but he couldn't stop the great flood of tears brimming over. 'I want my ma an' pa,' he sobbed.

As Cally stooped to console the youngster, Brad turned away to hide his own feelings; the sight of a youngster in distress always disturbed him profoundly.

'I was wonderin' how long it would be before it really hit him,' he said to Logan as Cally led the weeping boy away.

'Cally's a good girl,' Logan said when he and Brad were alone. 'She'll take care of him. She's looked after me since my wife died six months back. I reckon she'll make some guy a good wife soon.' He looked pointedly at Brad. 'You married?'

When Brad shook his head he sighed. 'Call me a sentimental old cuss but I reckon my Alice was the best thing that ever happened to me. During the war she gave me a reason to go on livin'.' He sighed. 'Brad, I'm old an' I'm tired. I guess I've been in the law game too long. What am I gonna do about this guy Solomon?'

'By all accounts he's too big fer one guy to handle,' Brad remarked.

'So when I write an' tell McNelly I need help, he sends you,' Logan said ironically.

'Not a moment too soon,' Brad said evenly, refusing to rise to the implied criticism. 'The guys I've met so far seemed real mean. When's Judge Bligh due here?'

Logan rose and consulted a calendar. 'A week today.'

'Maybe we'll have some more work fer him by then,' Brad said. 'What do you know about these guys I just brought in?'

Logan rolled two smokes and passed one to Brad.

'They're Jordan Tute's men,' he said, nodding towards the cells. 'He's one of Solomon's henchmen.'

'Jordan Tute?'

Brad fished out a well-thumbed notebook from his vest pocket. His brow furrowed as he studied it for a few minutes.

'It says here that amongst many other things, mostly cattle-rustling and horse-thievin', Jordan Tute is wanted fer the murder of an army quartermaster back in '69.'

'Was Tute supplying remounts?'

Brad nodded and blew a cloud of smoke at a fly on the ceiling. 'I guess he didn't like it when the quartermaster accused him of selling him stolen horses. The army always did have a long memory,' he mused.

Logan drew deeply. 'An' rightly so.' He looked keenly at Brad. 'Say, haven't we met somewhere before? Didn't you ride with Jeb Stuart?'

'Sure. Hampton's brigade.'

'I was with Robertson.' Logan grinned. 'Didn't we once get some of you boys out of a nasty scrape near Sharpsburg?'

Brad stared at Logan as the old memories came flooding back to life.

Of his frantic dash for safety hotly pursued by Union cavalry . . . of a wild rebel yell from the fringe of the dense woods . . . of the flurry of hooves . . . of the clash of sabres and the crack of revolvers . . . of men and horses screaming in agony . . . of the bodies of the dead and dying littering the dew-wet grass . . . of half a dozen riderless horses scurrying hither and thither . . .

A minor skirmish unrecorded in the annals of a mighty conflict but one that would hang forever on a canvas in the recesses of the minds of men like himself . . .

'Sure, Tex. I guess I owe you one.'

The two men's hands shot out and met in the firm clasp of former comrades-in-arms.

'Solomon's got another sidekick,' Logan said. 'Guy called Grimes. Built like a buffalo, with brains to match . . . '

'Grimes!' Brad exclaimed. 'I've heard about him. He and his brothers burned down the courthouse in Actonville. They murdered Judge Rawson an' raped his wife and daughter. The

Governor leaned on Captain McNelly real hard about that one. We've been lookin' for 'em fer well over a year now.'

Logan's face took on a worried expression. 'With guys like this runnin' amok it's no wonder nobody dare say anything.' He shook his head. 'This McDonald business is bad. I reckon there's big trouble brewin' for me. There's several small outfits like McDonald's along the border with Kell County. I reckon I oughta pay 'em a visit and check things out.'

Logan leaned forward to stub out his cigarette. 'Look Brad, this is strictly between you and me; I ain't told Cally this yet, but I'm a sick man. Doc Ryan told me only last week it's time I threw in my badge. Fact is, I've got a weak heart. Somehow I gotta bring myself to tell the folks here I'll stay on until they find someone else to do the job.'

'Guess that could be a mite difficult if there's trouble brewin',' Brad remarked.

Logan looked worried. 'Right. Look,

Brad, I ain't no quitter . . . '

'I know that,' Brad said. 'I suggest you stay right here while I go scout along the border.'

Logan looked relieved. 'Say, that's mighty good of you. Look, why don't you have dinner with me an' Cally tonight? I guess she needs some company for a change.'

5

Brad rose at sunrise and after brewing himself a quick mug of java, he saddled Blaze and rode out of town. The gargantuan meal of steak and eggs and apple-pie washed down with strong black coffee which Cally had cooked the previous evening would see him through most of the day.

By contrast, Tex Logan had eaten little and his naive attempt to match-make Brad with Cally failed dismally for his daughter was too concerned about his own lack of appetite. But although he enjoyed the meal, Brad was left with the uneasy feeling that the ageing lawman knew more about his physical condition than he was prepared to say . . .

The sheriff's daughter was no oil-painting. Her raw-boned features and rangy build and the way she chattered on ten to the dozen reminded him of his big sister, Beth, who'd brought him up as a youngster — and of a girl called Agnes he'd once met down Atlanta way at the tail-end of the war . . . a girl he'd let down so badly his cheeks burned at the memory of it. Instinctively he knew that, like Beth and Agnes, Cally was imbued with that peculiar toughness of spirit that marked all true frontier-women; but now and again she revealed the touching vulnerability and naivety of youth. Logan was right, she deserved a decent hardworking man who would take care of her. It was no wonder he was worried about her.

But as Brad rode along the trail which ran north parallel with the county line, Cally's eager talk and wistful gaze slipped out of his thoughts as he turned his mind to the job in hand. All the evidence so far showed that McNelly was right, the man who styled himself King Solomon was a man of overweening ambition. He was a bully who, like so many others, would one day overreach himself and bring about his own downfall. It was Brad's task to hasten the process . . .

He didn't need to look far. Logan's information was already out of date. Brad followed the route the lawman had given him, stopping by at three spreads at which he managed with great difficulty to persuade the frightened owners into admitting they'd had a recent visit from a band of outlaws whose description matched Ed Grimes and his gang. In each case, the plea was the same. 'Don't say it was us who told you, it's more than our lives are worth.'

'Does tha' know he robbed me of fifty head o' cattle,' John Summers told him when he reached his last port of call. He was an Englishman and spoke with a peculiar accent Brad had never heard before. His home was in some place called Yorkshire. It was late in the day and Brad gratefully accepted his offer of a bed for the night.

'Fifty steers ah've scratched and scraped for, mavericks culled from this damned catclaw,' Summers told him. 'But what could I do? If I'd tried to stop him they'd've shot me down, burned the ranch and taken the lot.'

'Are you willing to testify against him?' Brad asked the question for the fourth time.

'You mean stand up in court?' Summers shook his head. 'I'm sorry, Sergeant Saunders, tha's got to look after thissen. Wild horses wouldn't make me do that. No disrespect, but I've still got to live here after you've gone.'

Summers' wife spoke her fears privately to Brad as he saddled Blaze the following morning. She was a Texan, a tall handsome woman whose face was creased with anxiety.

'Those men scared the kids outa their wits, Sergeant Saunders,' she said in a low voice. 'I haven't said anything to my husband, but I . . . I didn't like the way the oldest man looked at me.'

Brad's heart went out to these simple people trying their best in an impossible situation. They had enough problems trying to make a living without the interference of men like Solomon, Tute and Grimes.

'Ah'm telling you straight, sergeant, if they keep on coming, we'll be ruined,' Summers said as he walked with Brad to the gate. 'Ah can't keep on paying out like this.'

'Don't you worry none,' Brad told him. 'By the time I've finished, Solomon and all who work for him are gonna get more'n they bargained for.'

Inside he wished he could feel more certain. He waved goodbye to the Summers family with the distinct feeling that McNelly had been right — this situation was going to need support from the rest of the company if it wasn't to get rapidly out of hand . . .

* * *

Something big was afoot, Abigail was sure of it. The level of activity at the ranch was higher than usual. During the afternoon the two rival gangs of her husband's henchmen had ridden in, hard-eyed men fronted by the frightening combination of Jordan Tute and Ed Grimes.

'Somethin's in the air,' Bannerman muttered.

He had met with her in the barn where she had gone to check on the condition of one of her string of thoroughbreds that had fallen sick.

'I've treated one of Tute's men for a gunshot wound. He told me a Texas Ranger did it,' Abigail replied. 'What's going on, Lee?'

Bannerman shook his head. 'Word's going round that a ranger has killed one of Tute's men. I wonder what's afoot?'

Abigail placed her hand on Bannerman's arm. 'I'll try and find out.'

Bannerman looked at her, puzzled. 'How will you do that?'

She put her finger to her lips. 'That's my secret . . .'

★   ★   ★

The atmosphere in Solomon's office at the Crown Ranch was tense. In the room next door Abigail pressed her ear close to a chink in the log wall just below the mantelpiece. If she concentrated hard she could hear every word that was spoken . . .

'You sayin' you want the bank in Dolores robbin'?'

It was Grimes' voice.

There was the rasp of a lucifer on sandpaper as he lit a cigarette.

'That's Eli Greensbee's bank ain't it? Say, ain't he your wife's father?'

Solomon uttered a high-pitched laugh. 'Yeah, it's time I taught that old buzzard a lesson. When I asked him for a loan once he treated me like I was dirt. I was never good enough to marry his daughter, he made that plain.'

'What's your wife gonna say about it?'

'What Abigail thinks is none of your business,' Solomon snapped irritably.

'You reckon you an' your boys can do it on your own?'

Abigail shuddered. It was the soulless voice of Jordan Tute speaking.

'I dunno,' Grimes said. 'I ain't never done a bank job before.'

'That's what I figured,' Tute said.

'Well I guess there's always a first time,' Solomon said brightly.

'That ranger might be there by now,' Grimes said.

'Oh come on, Ed, there's only one of 'em!' Solomon exploded. 'I heard about that business the other day. Four against one and he takes two prisoners? Goddammit, Jordan, what the hell were your boys playing at?'

'Red reckoned the guy was fast. When Clint went fer his gun he gave it to him, straight through the heart,' Tute replied.

The room fell silent as this piece of unpalatable information was digested.

'I want it we should hit that bank in Dolores as soon as possible,' Solomon said softly. 'Do it tomorrow. If you leave at first light you can hit it at closin' time. An' iffen you do meet up with

94

that ranger, *wipe him out.*'

'It'll be a pleasure, Tute said.

★ ★ ★

Abigail heard the jingle of spurs and the clump of riding-boots as the meeting broke up. She turned away from the wall and gasped as she saw the servant-girl standing in the open doorway.

'Peach!' she exclaimed. 'What do you want?'

The girl entered the room silently on bare feet.

'Mr Solomon says he won't be dining with you tonight.'

There was a note in her voice which Abigail took exception to. It seemed the girl was aware of the implied insult and was adding her own contempt to supplement it.

Abigail waited until Peach had left and then walked over to the window. Outside Grimes and his four brothers together with Tute and his eight men were coalescing into one group preparing to make the couple of hours ride into Kell — no doubt for an evening's hell-raising in a town where no good woman dared show her face.

She watched the fourteen outlaws ride out with a rising sense of desperation. Earl had been right just now. From the very beginning her father had always made no secret of the fact that he had no time for him. He'd helped Ben to get on his feet in the early years, but after his death and when she'd told him she was going to marry Earl he'd spoken his mind and they'd never seen each other since.

'You make your bed, my girl, and you lie on it,' had been his last word to her.

Now she had to face the bitter realization that her father's shrewd judgment of Earl's character had been right . . . was it possible she and her father could be reconciled?

Whether that was possible or not, she knew she must warn him that his bank was going to be raided.

How could she do it?

If only she could get word through to Sheriff Logan. If there was a ranger in the area, maybe he would help. But what could two men do against a surprise attack by the outlaw gangs?

Dusk was gathering as the outlaws cantered out of the gateway heading in the direction of Kell. Abigail winced. She was under no illusions; after a night of gambling, drinking and whoring in that hell-hole they would be off at first light on their deadly errand. From what she'd heard, they intended to arrive around closing-time — three o'clock. Somehow she must get a message through to the authorities in Dolores before they arrived . . .

As she drew away she caught sight of Lee Bannerman crossing the yard. That *hombre* wasn't a violent man, she knew, for he never carried a side-arm. He seemed to be a quiet introspective man who gave the impression he was carrying some impossible burden. Puzzled, she had questioned one of the hands about his brush with Grimes, for she was convinced that his behaviour in picking the quarrel had been quite out of character. He was in love with her, of that she was certain. He wasn't the first and hopefully he wouldn't be the last to do so. There had been a time when his admission of his feelings would have flattered and amused her, but right now it was an irksome complication she could well do without.

But then suddenly she had an idea.

Maybe she could persuade Lee Bannerman to help!

She picked up a black lace shawl from the back of a chair and drew it across her head and shoulders. Then she hurried out of the room and left the house, unaware of the soft footfall following her . . .

Bannerman was crouching, caressing the muzzle of the sick horse when she entered the barn. His pulse began to race when he saw her approaching.

'Why Abigail, what's the matter? You look as though you've seen a ghost!' he exclaimed as he straightened up.

She placed a finger to her lips and looked about her anxiously.

'Lee, I've just been listening to Earl talking with those men . . . '

Bannerman listened in silence as she told him of Solomon's plan.

'What can I do, Lee?' she whispered brokenly when she finished. 'Earl has got to be stopped. I know I have broken with my father but his life is in danger and I must do something. I cannot condone what my husband is doing any longer. He must be stopped. How can we warn the sheriff in Dolores?'

Bannerman frowned. 'That ranger may be there by now.'

'But what can he and the sheriff do if they are taken by surprise? They must be warned so they can get others to help them . . . '

In her agitation she drew closer to him. 'Oh, Lee, I am so worried about my father. We must do something!'

'Like what?' Bannerman said help-lessly.

'Can't you send one of the men to warn the sheriff?'

'I would if I had a man I knew I could trust, but they are all in Solomon's pay . . . '

She pressed closer to him.

'Then go yourself! Do it, for my sake, Lee. Earl has got to be stopped.'

Bannerman felt himself weakening, but fear held him back.

Go himself — with a ranger waiting? He might just as well put his head in a noose!

Abigail clung to him. 'Oh Lee, please help me.'

He pushed her away roughly, his mind in a turmoil. 'You don't understand, Abigail. I gotta job here, I can't just ride out when I feel like it . . . '

As Abigail drew close to him, the scent of her perfume made his head reel, breaking the slender hold he kept over his resolution.

'A man like you shouldn't be working for Earl Solomon,' she said. 'There can't be a decent future for you here. I think you know that yourself.'

'But you said yourself, Earl is your husband . . . '

Abigail spat on the floor of the barn.

'My husband? When was he last my husband? I wish I had never married him.'

Losing all inhibition, she slipped into Bannerman's arms.

'Kiss me, Lee,' she whispered, 'before you go.'

As their lips met, a slight noise behind them broke them apart.

'What was that?' Abigail exclaimed in alarm.

'Maybe it was one of the horses stirring,' Bannerman said, stepping forward to investigate. 'Although I swear it was a footfall.'

Abigail entwined her arms about his neck and kissed him passionately.

'You will go to Dolores?' she said.

'OK,' Bannerman said resignedly. 'I'll go.'

★ ★ ★

The outlaws hit Kell with a chorus of blood-curdling rebel yells. They jumped off their horses and spilled into the saloons and whorehouses. Grimes was about to follow his brothers into Micah's when Tute held him by the arm.

'Ed, you an' me's gotta talk,' Tute said in his toneless voice.

'What about?'

'This bank job. We gotta decide who's doin' what.'

Grimes nodded. 'OK, let's do that.'

The two men entered the saloon.

'Whiskey,' Grimes ordered the barman. Armed with the bottle and two glasses he went over to where Tute was sitting alone at a previously crowded table.

Grimes poured two drinks and the two men downed them in silence.

'Well?' Grimes said as he poured two more.

'D'you reckon your boys are up to this job?'

As Grimes downed number two he

felt the fire rise in his cheeks.

'Just what do you mean by that?' he demanded.

'Well, you seemed a mite uneasy when Solomon raised it.'

Grimes poured number three. 'It ain't no problem, Jordan. We just ride in, hold up the tellers an' make off with the cash. The more I think about it the easier it gets.'

'That's just where you're wrong. Dolores is a big town — much bigger than Kell. The bank's plumb in the centre. Whichever of us does the job needs the other to cover his back.'

Grimes pondered over his glass of amber liquid. If Jordan Tute was bothered, maybe the job wasn't the pushover he'd thought it was going to be. And he was one down without Frank.

'So, what you're saying is that one of us goes in, and the other keeps watch?'

'Somethin' like that,' said Tute. 'Thing is, we gotta decide who does what.'

He produced a pack of cards. 'Highest goes in?'

Grimes nodded.

He waited while Tute shuffled the pack in his prehensile fingers and laid them on the table.

'You first.'

As Grimes leaned forward, for the first time in his life he felt queasy. A bead of sweat burst forth on his forehead. This wasn't just a question of terrorizing a lone rancher, it was the big-time. If he went in and bungled it there would be more than his reputation at stake, it could cost him his life . . . He drew a card and laid it on the table.

Three of Clubs.

Could be low enough! Relief flooded through him. Hanging back while Jordan's boys took the risk suddenly seemed like the best deal . . .

Tute's face was impassive as his hand hovered like a claw over the pack.

Grimes leaned forward eagerly like a man about to be reprieved from the gallows.

Tute cut and turned a card.

Two of Diamonds.

As Tute recovered the pack and rose from the table a ghost of a smile crossed his thin lips.

'I guess I'll be right behind yuh, Ed,' he said as he strode towards the door.

Grimes picked up the whiskey bottle and went in search of his brothers.

'What gives?' Zeke asked. He had his arm wrapped round the shoulders of a grinning honky-tonk.

'Best save your strength, Zeke. Come first light we're ridin' into Dolores with Tute an' his boys. We're gonna rob the bank.'

'Hell's teeth!' Jud said. 'We ain't never done no bank job before. Who's gonna knock on the door?'

'Guess we drew the short straw. Is Frank still sick?'

'Yep,' Curt answered. 'He says he needs a coupla days before he's right.'

'Then we're gonna need someone to hold the horses,' Grimes said. 'Way I see it, we don't wanna be one short.'

Zeke nodded. 'What about one of Tute's men?'

'No,' Grimes said. 'I don't trust him. He says he's gonna back us but if things go wrong I ain't convinced.'

His brothers nodded.

'We could use the kid,' Curt said tentatively.

Grimes shook his head.

'Aw, c'mon now, Lu, we only want someone to hold the horses. Where's the harm in that? The kid can go back to the ranch once the job's done.'

'That ain't the point. I don't want him involved, he's too young.'

'There ain't no need fer him to fight,' Jud said persuasively. 'He don't need to pack a gun.'

'Sure, sure, no need at all,' Curt backed him up.

'I'd rather have one of the family with me than one of Tute's men,' Zeke growled.

'I told you I don't wanna involve the kid,' Grimes said stubbornly.

'Why wrap him in cotton wool?' Jud

remarked. 'He's keen as mustard. You gotta let the boy have his head sooner or later.'

'Who else is there to hold the horses?' Curt said with a shrug.

'Solomon has promised to cut us in when this job's over,' Grimes said, changing the subject.

Zeke cock-a-doodled with laughter. But the expression on his eldest brother's face brought his face straight abruptly.

'What's so funny 'bout that?' Grimes demanded.

'You reckon Solomon's gonna give somethin' away? Come on, Ed, pigs might fly an' monkeys chew tobacco.'

Grimes scowled. Zeke had an uncomfortably direct way of speaking his mind. And in his heart, he knew he was right.

'Aw, come on, Lu, he's joshin' you,' Zeke continued. 'Anyway, what's with all this hankering to be a businessman? Quit talkin' moonshine. Nobody ever gave us an even break.

We're outlaws, like it or not.'

'Face it, Lu, sooner or later we're gonna have to cut loose from Solomon,' Jud said slowly. 'Jordan Tute's his right-hand man. Where does that leave you?'

'Is Joel in, then?' Curt demanded.

'OK. And seeing as it was your idea, you an' Jud can go over to the ranch an' fetch him,' Grimes said resignedly.

★　★　★

Bannerman left Abigail, his mind a jumble of emotions. She was using him; he was aware of it and yet he was so in thrall he was totally unable to refuse. Yet once he left the Crown Ranch he knew he was laying himself wide open to Solomon's denunciation of him to the rangers. And once she knew of his past, where would that leave him in the eyes of Abigail? He grimaced. Did it matter? There was no way could he be certain that Abigail would turn to him if her marriage to

Earl Solomon fell through.

If the ranger was present in Dolores matters could all come to a head sooner rather than later. He hadn't needed Solomon to remind him that those guys had pocket-books crammed with long lists of names and they had even longer memories — which was why he'd hidden away in Kell under an assumed name.

But it was too late now, he'd made his decision. He planned on leaving when the ranch was quiet. Which meant shortly after midnight.

As top-screw, he bunked down in a small room separate from the hands. Dusk was gathering and he paused to roll a smoke, nodding to two of the hands chatting on the stoop. Best try to convey the impression that nothing was amiss. Once inside he gathered his shaving-tackle, his spare set of clothes and other odds and ends and crammed them into the warbag he kept stashed under the bed. On completing this task, he was left with a couple of hours to kill.

He left his rooms and went into the bunkhouse. One guy was playing a jew's harp. Some of the others were lying on their bunks thumbing through dime novels, some were writing letters with studious concentration. Young Joel lay fast asleep. A card-school attracted Bannerman.

'Mind if I sit in?'

The men looked surprised, but none declined. Bannerman joined them, acutely aware that he had gone down in their estimation since that fracas with Grimes.

He sat in on a game of monte. He'd never played with the men before, preferring to keep himself to himself. One of the big ranch-bosses in The Panhandle he'd once worked for had forbidden gambling of any kind, but Solomon was no such martinet. All the same Bannerman made his own rule that the stakes were kept at a nominal level and ensured the hands respected it.

As time passed, Bannerman could sense the tenseness in the atmosphere. The men had seen the outlaws come and go and they figured something big was in the wind.

Suddenly the bunkhouse door burst open and two men walked in. Bannerman recognized the Grimes twins, Jud and Curt.

'We've come fer the boy,' Curt said.

By now Joel was wide awake, staring goggle-eyed.

'You're to come with us,' Jud ordered. 'An' don't ask questions.'

'You walk out an' you're finished here, boy,' Bannerman warned.

'You think I care?' Joel sneered jubilantly as he pulled on his shirt and pants. 'I need your advice like I need a hole in the head. You prate worse than a preacher-man.'

'OK, it's your life,' Bannerman said with a shrug.

'You bet it is,' Joel said with a grin. 'Me, I'm gonna ride with my brothers. See you in hell, Bannerman.'

Peach knocked on the door of her employer's office and waited for his peremptory command to enter.

Fear and resignation gripped her as he smiled, saying, 'Come in, my dear,' in the honeyed tone he reserved for all his amorous conquests.

He rose from his desk, came round to her, and seized her roughly in his arms. It was useless to resist. The first time she had fought and he had beaten her senseless. The war had been fought but she was still a slave. One day perhaps, she would take her revenge . . .

★ ★ ★

It was gone midnight when the card-school broke up. Bannerman collected his modest winnings and retired to his room where he waited impatiently for half an hour before he could be sure everyone was asleep. Then he picked up his warbag and made his way stealthily out of the bunkhouse and into the moonlit yard.

After a brief recce, he crossed the yard and entered the barn. He found his sorrel, saddled it and led the animal towards the door. As he opened it, he caught sight of a shadowy figure approaching.

Bannerman didn't believe in ghosts. He let go of the sorrel's bridle and eased forward, peering into the gloom to see who it was.

'Abigail!' he exclaimed as she joined him inside the barn.

She put a slim finger to her lips to silence him.

'I'm coming with you, Lee.'

'You can't do that!' he exclaimed.

He glanced down and saw she was wearing her riding-habit. She was a competent rider; he had no doubt about her ability to complete the long overnight journey to Dolores.

'I thought we agreed that I should go,' he said. 'You didn't say you wanted to come. But do you know what you're doing? If you come with me, you are leaving your husband . . . '

'My husband? Pah!' Abigail spat on the ground so viciously Bannerman's horse skitted. 'Do you think I don't know what that pig is doing? Tonight he is with that serving-girl, Peach. I heard them in one of the bedrooms together . . . he is making love to her.'

Bannerman's blood ran cold. This was a side of Abigail he hadn't imagined existed.

Hell hath no fury like a woman scorned, his grandmother used to say. She was right, too, Solomon's behaviour had turned Abigail from a good woman into a spitting, vengeful hellcat.

'There's nothing to keep me here,' she said. 'I'm coming with you to Dolores.'

'Solomon won't let you go that easy,' Bannerman said. 'He'll come looking for you.'

'I'll be safe with my father. He owns a ranch where he employs a lot of men. I can stay there. Now please, help me saddle my horse.'

With a shrug Bannerman did as she asked. A few minutes later he opened the barn door and led his sorrel out into the yard. At his signal, Abigail followed him leading her most treasured possession, a magnificent Spanish mare, a gift from her first husband. They walked the horses across the yard to the gate which Bannerman contrived to open silently. Once they were through it, he helped her into the saddle.

'Abigail, are you sure this is what you want?' Bannerman said in a low voice.

'Yes, I'm sure,' she replied stonily.

6

Brad was wolfing a meal of beans, bacon and steak washed down with a beer at the Rearing Horse Restaurant on Main Street, Dolores, when the door opened and Cally came rushing in.

'Why Cally, what's the matter?' he drawled. 'More bad news?'

'You betcha! Pa says will you come over to his office pronto!'

Brad wiped his mouth hastily on his napkin.

'That was one helluva nice steak,' he said wistfully.

Cally grabbed his arm. 'C'mon, c'mon, this is urgent. Let's go. I'll cook you another steak later.'

'Mind tellin' me what this is all about?' he enquired as they left the restaurant.

'There's no time,' she replied.

The girl almost ran him down the

street to her father's office. She ran ahead of him up the steps onto the sidewalk and flung open the door.

'I got him!' she announced.

'Thank God!' Logan exclaimed, starting out of his chair. He turned to face the woman standing beside his desk. 'Brad, have I gotta surprise for you. This lady here is Mrs Abigail Solomon.'

'*Mrs* Solomon!'

'Don't look so flabbergasted, Sergeant Saunders,' Abigail said calmly.

Brad shook his head in disbelief. Somehow he hadn't reckoned on the King having a Queen. Although her riding-habit and face were smeared with dust and she looked tired after her overnight ride, it still didn't disguise the fact that Abigail Solomon was a very beautiful woman.

'Please call me Abigail, Sergeant Saunders.'

As he removed his hat to acknowledge her, Brad missed the flash of interest in Cally's eyes as she looked at the tall stranger standing beside her.

'And this is Lee Bannerman, Solomon's ranch foreman,' Logan completed the introductions.

'*Was* Solomon's foreman,' Bannerman corrected him.

As the two men shook hands Brad noticed Bannerman didn't pack a gun, but he showed signs of recently having been in a fight. High on his left cheek there was a noticeably livid scar. Now how had he come by that?

'Mrs Solomon tells me that she's overheard her husband instructing Grimes and Tute to rob the bank here in Dolores,' Logan said quietly.

'So why your concern?' Brad asked Abigail pointedly.

'Because I don't approve of what my husband is doing,' she flashed back at him, plainly put out by the bluntness of his manner.

'Perhaps I should explain that Mrs Solomon's father is president of the bank,' Logan said.

'From what she overheard,' Bannerman

said, 'I reckon these guys are aiming to hit the bank around closing-time.'

Logan pulled out a watch from his vest pocket. His face was unnaturally red and his breathing was coming in quick short breaths. 'That's in less'n an hour's time.'

'I gather my father isn't in town,' Abigail said. 'We must tell the chief clerk to close the bank. They can't do anything if they find the shutters up.'

Brad pondered. This talk was way ahead of his thinking. Solomon's wife defecting with his ranch foreman? It seemed a strange alliance. Were they telling the truth or was Solomon setting up some kind of trap?

Suddenly he made up his mind.

'Well, I guess we'll fix a welcome for these guys.'

'I'll go and warn the chief clerk,' Logan said.

'No,' Brad said. 'I want to keep the bank open.'

'As a bait?' Bannerman said, cocking one eye quizzically.

Brad nodded. This guy was pretty shrewd.

'Now wait a minute, I will not have my father's employees put at risk!' Abigail exclaimed.

'There won't be any risk — not fer them anyway,' Brad said. 'How many men will Solomon send, d'you reckon?' he asked Bannerman.

'Grimes has five brothers including the kid who's just joined 'em. Tute has around a dozen gunslingers on his pay-roll, but since you came he's down to eight fit men.'

'So we're lookin' at maybe thirteen or fourteen.' Brad turned to Logan. 'How many deputies can you swear in?'

Logan shook his head. 'Be lucky if I get half a dozen at this short notice — especially when they find Solomon is behind this business. There's a lotta hot air about takin' action, but very little gets done when the chips are down.'

Brad gave a non-committal nod.

'I know the guys you want, Pa. I'll go round 'em up,' Cally said. 'You stay here, Abigail. I'll be right back.'

'For what it's worth, I can't see Grimes and Tute co-operatin',' Bannerman said. 'They never did see eye to eye. Grimes always figures he's second fiddle to Tute in Solomon's eyes. Way I see it, Grimes and his brothers will rob the bank and Tute and his men might cover 'em — after a fashion.'

Brad pondered for a moment. This was disappointing, he'd wanted the chance to take both of Solomon's henchmen out in one move, but he was committed now . . .

'Get your deputies to clear the street,' he told Logan. 'Keep it low-key, we don't want the town in an uproar. Put a coupla guys in the upper storey of the saloon opposite the bank and have the rest cover both ends of the street.'

'Where are you gonna be?' Logan demanded.

'Inside. However many there are, I reckon only two of 'em will enter the building.'

'OK,' Logan muttered. He rose,

strapped on his gunbelt and strode to the door. He paused in the doorway. 'If I'm gonna be in charge outside, who's gonna be inside the bank with you?'

'Wasn't figuring on anyone else,' Brad replied.

Bannerman stepped forward. 'I'll come with you.'

'If you do, you're gonna need a weapon,' Brad said, eyeing Bannerman's deficiency.

'Sheriff Logan'll fix me up, I guess,' Bannerman replied.

'Sure, sure,' Logan said. He opened his desk, found a key and tossed it to him. 'Help yourself,' he said, pointing to the gun-rack. 'I'll deputize you along with the rest.'

Bannerman selected a pair of well-worn Army Colts, checked the actions and stuffed them into his belt.

'You sure you're gonna be up to this?' Brad muttered out of the corner of his mouth as they made for the door.

'Just because a man don't pack a

gun, it don't mean he ain't never used one,' Bannerman replied bleakly.

* * *

Half an hour later, Brad was crouching underneath the solid oak counter of the bank, aware of the tense expression on the face of Lee Bannerman, who had adopted a similar posture, five yards away.

Who was this guy? He'd had no time to check him out. For all he knew he was exposing himself to a highly dangerous situation with someone he knew nothing about. He'd only Bannerman's word he could handle a situation like this. He grimaced, it was too late to do anything about it now, so to pass the time he took out his watch from his vest pocket and squinted at it. Five minutes to three . . .

Above him, the chief clerk shuffled his feet nervously against the legs of his high stool as he pretended to be adding the figures up in a ledger.

Four minutes to go!

Logan had signalled that he and his deputies were in position. For the hundredth time Brad went over the plan in his mind, searching for flaws that it was now too late to rectify.

Three minutes!

The tension in the oven-hot office rose a notch. The chief clerk was a peace-loving man, anxious to go home as usual to his wife and family; he had remained at his post at Brad's request in order to create an air of normality. Brad had given him his assurance that he could leave the moment the outlaws arrived.

But the demon of doubt was dancing a jig inside his guts, the hairs on his forearms bristled, and his mouth was as parched as an arroyo after a summer's drought.

A trickle of sweat rolled down his back. It was the waiting that did it. It always did. It reminded him of those tense moments during the war before a battle began. The moment before reason yielded to the most primeval instinct with a man . . . self-preservation.

Slowly as the seconds ticked away, his anxiety yielded to a deep sense of inner calm. He was older now, wiser in the ways of the world which had only just discovered what every inhabitant of the American West had always known instinctively — that only the fittest survive.

Two minutes!

Brad took out his Peacemaker and checked the loads. He noticed Bannerman was doing the same with the Colts Logan had loaned him.

One minute!

Outside a wagon rumbled to a halt. The final customer, a woman, bade the chief clerk good-day and left. Brad had instructed the man not to lock the doors immediately in case the outlaws were late — but he needn't have worried. As the minute hand flicked onto three o'clock, he lifted his head above the counter. Through the window he could see Sheriff Logan waving the prearranged signal with his bandanna in the upper storey window of the saloon opposite.

King Solomon's men had arrived . . .

* * *

Grimes rode shoulder to shoulder with Tute at the head of their men as they cantered into Dolores. Tucking in close behind at the rear was the youngest and newest recruit to outlawry — Joel.

'This place seems awful quiet,' Zeke muttered as they rode along the street past the *jacals* of the town's Mexican quarter. After half a mile or so, these gave way to a line of business premises — stores, a gunsmith, a saddler, two livery stables and half a dozen saloons, several cheap lodging-houses — even a hotel — until they reached the spot where the stone-built courthouse stood and the commercial heart of Dolores was beating gently in the ferocious heat of the midday sun.

Tute's dust-smeared lips curled back in a cross between a smile and a sneer. It gave him the appearance of a rabid dog.

'You still feelin' edgy, Zeke?' he said, with what his associates recognized as a sly grin.

Zeke shifted uneasily in his saddle. He released one hand from the reins to rasp his black-stubbled cheeks throughtfully as his dun slowed to a walk.

'Place as big as this should be much busier,' he observed.

Grimes glanced shrewdly across at his brother.

'What you sayin', Zeke?'

'Dunno.' Zeke hunched his shoulders under his jacket and glanced round speculatively. 'It just don't feel right somehow.'

His brother Jud grinned. 'Aw c'mon, Zeke, quit talkin' like an old woman . . . '

'Hold it!' Grimes snapped.

As they slowed, the twins Jud and

Curt crowded in behind them, their horses snorting.

'Well, are we goin' in or not?' Curt demanded. His hand rested on the butt of a long-handled axe strapped to his saddle. 'Don't tell me I've toted this damn thing all the way from Kell fer nuthin'.'

Grimes ignored him. He took out his watch.

'Nearly three,' he muttered. His hooded eyes surveyed the empty street, taking in a cat dozing in the shadow of the sidewalk and a passing dog, its pads scuffing the dust as it trotted purposefully across the street.

'If we're goin' through with this, we'd best get on with it. They'll be putting the shutters up soon,' Curt said.

'We're only one block away now,' Tute said. 'You won the draw, Ed, I guess it's all yours. Good luck. We'll stay hereabouts. Me an' my boys'll back yuh should you need it.'

Grimes nodded and led his brothers clear of Tute's men.

A heavily-laden wagon came trundling towards them and halted in the street in front of the bank entrance. The teamster jumped down from his seat, paused to light his pipe and walked towards the dry-goods store holding a manifest.

They hung back, until the man had entered the store and then cantered forward, finally coming to a halt a few yards short of the bank entrance.

As they arrived, a woman customer left the bank. They waited until she crossed the street before Grimes and Zeke dismounted. To a casual observer they looked no different to any other bunch of cowhands who had just ridden into town.

'OK, boys, you know what to do,' Grimes said. 'Zeke and me'll go in at the front and we'll meet you inside. Joel, you have the horses ready in the back road.'

Joel nodded as he collected the reins and, accompanied by Jud and Curt, led the horses down a side-alley which led off the main street to the rear of the bank.

'Let's go,' Grimes snapped.

Just as if they were customers, Zeke strolled alongside his brother along the sidewalk until they came to the swing-door which led into the foyer of the bank . . .

★   ★   ★

As Brad tugged at the hem of his coat, the chief clerk slid off his high stool and disappeared through the door leading to the office like a bolting rabbit. As Brad rose to his feet to take the man's place behind the counter, out of the corner of his eye he was aware of Bannerman doing the same.

Suddenly the massive bulk of Grimes darkened the doorway. When he saw Brad he took one step further into the room to allow Zeke in behind him and paused, puzzled for a moment.

'Lucifer Grimes!' Bannerman exclaimed under his breath.

'You're under arrest, Grimes,' Brad said quietly. 'I got men posted outside. You're surrounded.'

From an initial expression of intense surprise, the two men's eyes narrowed when they saw the gleam of the silver badge which proclaimed Brad's office.

'Hell's teeth, it's the ranger!' Zeke said hoarsely.

Brad was already ducking behind the counter as Grimes' gun appeared in his hand with unbelievable speed and spat a lick of flame. The blast sounded shockingly loud in the confined space of the office and the slug smashed into a picture of Eli Greensbee, the bank president, hanging on the wall, showering Brad with glass shards.

The initial surprise over, the two outlaws turned and ran for the door.

As Brad and Bannerman vaulted simultaneously over the counter, Zeke turned and loosed off a snapshot. Bannerman swore bitterly as he dropped one of his weapons and clutched at his upper right arm.

'Looks like Grimes drew the short straw,' Bannerman shouted at Brad as he ripped off his bandanna and used it to try to staunch the flow of blood from his flesh-wound.

As Brad hastily tied the knot, firing began outside.

'You gonna be OK?'

Bannerman nodded. 'I'll live. I wonder where the others are?'

'Sounds like Logan's got those two pinned down. You stay here and cover the main entrance. I'll go upstairs and take a look-see.'

Leaving Bannerman, Brad raced up the stairs with giant strides and a few seconds later emerged on the balcony overlooking the street.

He looked on the scene below with grim satisfaction.

Sheriff Logan had posted his men well. He and one of his deputies had opened up from the window of the saloon opposite, their Winchesters pouring a stream of lead into the elegant facade of the bank below. The two outlaws who had entered the bank must be well and truly pinned down behind a goods-wagon. But where were the rest of Grimes' brothers?

Brad's first inkling that things were going badly wrong came when a slug whined past his head.

As he ducked, he snatched a look. A large group of horsemen had pulled up further along the street. Already he could see them unsheathing rifles from their scabbards. They must be Tute and his men, covering Grimes — just as Bannerman thought they might . . .

Once dismounted, they fanned out, using the cover afforded by the deep shade of the railed boardwalk, from where they opened fire on Brad and the two deputies Logan had posted on the upper-floor balcony of an hotel further along the street.

Brad knew it was useless for him to remain here, he was hopelessly out-ranged and outgunned. Ducking low to avoid flying splinters of wood, he saw one of Logan's deputies pitch forward from the balcony of the hotel into the street. Moments later one of Tute's men was hit and slumped over the rail of the sidewalk like a rag doll.

The firefight below him was unceasing in its ferocity. It seemed clear to Brad that the outlaws in front of the bank would have to surrender or be killed. So why were they still resisting?

Where the hell were the rest of the Grimes brothers?

He could have kicked himself as the answer dawned on him. Ducking low, he withdrew from the balcony and raced back down the stairs, two at a time, with the intention of warning Bannerman that he was about to be taken in the rear . . .

★   ★   ★

Further down the street, Tute and his men discovered it was death to move closer to the bank, even by edging along the deep shade of the boardwalk. The bodies of two of his men now lay dead in the street, a mute testimony to the accurate shooting from Logan's remaining deputy in the balcony of the hotel.

'I reckon Grimes an' his boys have walked into a trap,' Tute muttered.

'What we gonna do, boss?' one of his men asked him. 'Shall we rush 'em?'

'Not on your life,' Tute said with a snarl. 'Best thing we can do is get the hell outa here.'

Beside him, a man cursed and backed off as a slug whined past his head. Tute loosed off two speculative shots at the hotel balcony with his Winchester before pausing to reload. Further along the street he could see Grimes and Zeke struggling to hold their position behind the cover offered by the wheels of a wagon parked near the bank entrance.

'What the hell are they playin' at?' one of his men muttered.

Tute gave a wry smile. It was some kind of trap, for sure. Two Grimes brothers were in a hell of a tight spot.

With any luck, they would be wiped out and Solomon would make him his sole business partner . . .

'OK, boys,' he said, 'let's go.'

★ ★ ★

'What the hell is Tute playin' at?' Grimes snarled after he and Zeke had bellied the ground behind the wagon. 'We're pinned down here. I knew I couldn't trust the sonofabitch.'

He leaned round a wheel as he spoke and loosed off a couple of shots at the saloon window. He swore fluently as his temerity was rewarded with a hail of lead from Logan and his deputy.

'At least we know why they was expectin' us,' Zeke said bitterly. 'That skunk Bannerman was backin' the ranger.'

'We ain't got no place to go except back through the bank,' Grimes growled. 'Where's Jud an' Curt?'

Suddenly there was a burst of shots in the bank behind them.

'That'll be them breakin' in,' Grimes said. 'I'm goin' back inside. Maybe I can take them two by surprise.'

'You reckon?' Zeke was highly conscious of a numb feeling in his left buttock where a bullet had creased him.

'We ain't through yet,' Grimes said. 'You stay here and keep these guys' heads down while I make a break for it. Once I've linked up with Jud an' Curt I'll be back.'

Zeke checked the loads in his Colt and settled into position . . .

'OK?'

Zeke nodded, and as Sheriff Logan raised his head to peer cautiously out of the window, he fanned the hammer and let loose a fusillade of shots . . .

★　★　★

Brad arrived at the foot of the stairs just as the rear door of the bank was beginning to yield to the repeated blows of Curt's axe. Splinters filled the air as the assault reached a climax. As the door fell off its hinges, Brad emptied his gun into the cloud of dust swirling in the yard.

His boldness was rewarded for it yielded a howl of pain and gave him enough respite to draw back and reload. His hope was that his bold move would confuse the attackers, making them believe there was more than just one waiting for them.

He held back as bullets came pouring through the doorway like a swarm of bees. It was clear that the outlaws weren't going to give up easily. In the acrid smell of the rolling clouds of smoke that filled the passageway, Brad felt the first twinge of uncertainty.

What the hell was going on?

He emptied his weapon once more and withdrew. As he crouched to reload, the door leading into the main office swung open.

He half rose, expecting to see Bannerman.

But it wasn't the ex-Crown Ranch top-screw, it was the squat bulk of Lucifer Grimes!

Brad's weapon was empty. His only advantage was that the outlaw hadn't seen him . . . as he leapt to his feet another hail of bullets swept through the doorway, forcing Grimes to dodge back into the office.

'Jud, Curt, hold your fire!' Grimes bawled.

In the silence that followed, Brad hurled himself across the passage at the unsuspecting outlaw, his gun hacking and clubbing . . .

His unexpected assault drove Grimes backwards into the bank office. The big outlaw fought back but Brad had seized the initiative and no way was he going to forgo it. He whipped up the butt of his Colt under Grimes' jaw. The outlaw's head snapped back and he fell back against Bannerman, knocking him over like a skittle in a bowling-alley. In the resulting confusion, Grimes broke clear.

Although hampered by the wound in his arm, Bannerman was still fighting. He recovered quickly and one of his borrowed Colts winked spurts of flame at the shadowy figure of Grimes retreating through the rolling clouds of smoke.

'You go after him, I'll stay here and hold 'em off!' Bannerman shouted. He tossed his second weapon to Brad who seized it without question for he realized that his own preoccupation with Grimes had taken his mind off the attack from behind.

He brushed past Bannerman and raced for the office door, firing on the run, but by the time he reached the door to his chagrin no-one was there . . . and as he turned he tripped and fell, struck his head, and his consciousness dissolved into a shower of fiery sparks . . .

★ ★ ★

From the upper storey of the saloon, Sheriff Logan swore under his breath as he saw Grimes make his bid to get back inside the bank.

He sighted his Winchester and saw the bullets kick up the dust in the street round the outlaw's heels as he disappeared from view.

'Will someone tell me what the hell is going on?' he roared.

'The rest of Grimes' boys must be round the back of the bank,' his deputy replied.

'Where did the rest of 'em get to?'

The deputy peered through the broken window.

'It looks like Tute and his men are pullin' out,' he said.

'We'll see about that,' Logan said. 'Look, there's only one left in front of the bank. You keep him covered while I go take a look down yonder.'

Logan reloaded his Winchester and left the room. By the time he had reached the foot of the staircase, his heart was thumping so much he had to stop and pause for breath. Sheer will-power drove him on and when he had recovered his normal breathing he left the saloon through a door at the rear. He traversed a narrow alley along the back of the business premises which ran parallel to the main street before taking a turning which brought him in sight of the outlaws who were making ready to leave.

Flattening himself against a wall he edged along until he caught sight of the lanky figure of Jordan Tute. The outlaw was standing slightly apart from the rest of his men.

'Tute, I'm arrestin' you . . . ' Logan shouted. It seemed like an iron band was clasping his chest and his breath came in great gasps as he spoke.

The cold expression on the outlaw's face changed to the snarl of a cornered wolf. Mesmerized, the lawman froze for one stomach-churning second before Tute's arm moved with unbelievable speed . . . then his gun appeared and was spitting flame.

Logan's mouth opened in a silent

scream of agony as the bullet caught
him, spinning him round like a
top. Then he crumpled and fell
heavily against a garbage-can in the
alley . . .

7

Only a few minutes had elapsed, but it seemed like hours, before Brad came round. As after any battle, the silence seemed uncanny now that the firing had stopped. The hazy shape of Bannerman appeared through the swirling smoke and despite the handicap of his wounded arm, he bent down to help Brad to his feet.

'What happened?' Brad muttered as he felt gingerly at the lump on his head.

'They got away,' Bannerman said laconically. 'Neither of us was in a position to stop them, I guess.'

Brad cursed long and loud. 'The back door! I should've figured they might come in that way.'

'No reason for you to think that,' Bannerman said with a shrug. 'Let's go take a look outside.'

The prospect of a big butcher's bill

144

was writ large in Brad's mind as the two men stepped cautiously out into the street. Several townsfolk were already appearing, white-faced, talking in low tones, obviously stunned at the ferocity of the gun-battle.

Two corpses lay further down the street. Doc Ryan was already doing his job, a black-clad figure hovering for a few moments beside each body like the Angel of Death.

'They look like two of Tute's boys,' Bannerman muttered as they approached.

'Looks like the birds have flown,' Brad said disgustedly as he watched Logan's deputies emerging from their hiding-places. They were exchanging the relieved banter of men proud to have taken part in a dangerous enterprise from which, apart from one of their number, they had emerged unscathed.

'Say, Sergeant Saunders, didn't we give them guys a roastin'?' one of the deputies called out.

Brad responded with a curt nod. He was aware that in every action the proportion of hits to shots fired was usually very low, but this result disappointed him. He was acutely aware that if he'd had the backing of his fellow-rangers things would have been very different. As it was, the Grimes brothers together with Tute and most of his men had escaped.

'Where's Sheriff Logan?' he asked of one of the deputies.

'Back in his office, waitin' on Doc Ryan,' came the reply. 'He took one in the shoulder.'

'Tell him I'll be along in five minutes,' Doc Ryan said. He looked at Brad and Bannerman. 'You guys go along to the sheriff's office,' he ordered. 'I'll check you out over there.'

Bannerman followed Brad along the sidewalk until they came to Logan's office. They paused beside the door. Brad held out his hand to Bannerman.

'Thanks fer backing me,' he said.

Bannerman's face broke into a wry

smile as they shook hands. 'I was beginnin' to think you'd forgotten I was there,' he said drily.

Cally appeared in the doorway, her face full of concern.

'Where's Doc Ryan? I'm worried. Pa's hurt real bad.'

'He'll be along soon,' Brad told her.

'Oh, *you've* been wounded as well!' she cried.

'Don't fuss, they're only grazes,' Brad said.

They found Abigail waiting inside.

'Thank God you're safe!' she exclaimed when she saw the two men.

Logan was sitting in his chair, holding a blood-soaked towel against his shoulder, his face grey with pain.

'I tried to stop Tute, but he shot me,' he told Brad. 'Grimes and his brothers got away.'

'We did get one of 'em,' Cally said. 'He's under lock and key with the other two you brought in.'

'He was holdin' the horses round the back of the bank. He must've got knocked down when they rode off,' Logan said through clenched teeth.

'I want a word with that guy,' Brad said grimly.

Cally picked up the keys and led the way along the corridor to the cells.

'Go easy, he's only a kid, Brad,' she said as she unlocked the door.

Brad glanced sharply at her. It was a remarkably charitable statement to make in view of what had just happened, but somehow it was no more than he would have expected of her.

Bannerman stayed behind Brad as he stepped inside the cell and when Brad motioned Cally to leave she gave him the keys and withdrew.

'When are we gonna be charged, mister?' Al Quater asked plaintively. 'My ass is gettin' sore from sittin' here.'

'When I'm good and ready,' Brad snapped.

The youngster's eyes met his with a mixture of arrogance and defiance which changed to incredulity when he saw Bannerman.

'What the hell are you doin' here?' he exclaimed. He grinned and snapped his fingers. 'Hey, I got it. You must've run off with Mrs Solomon . . . '

'I've had enough of you,' Bannerman growled.

The kid's smile disappeared as the ex-Crown Ranch foreman's good arm came up in a roundhouse swipe and hit him across the face with the flat of his hand with a crack like a rifle-shot.

Brad made no attempt to intervene. If the kid had to learn the hard way, then so be it.

'You'll pay fer that,' Joel shouted, rubbing his stinging cheek. 'You wait while I see Lu.'

'You could have a mighty long wait, boy,' Brad drawled.

'Who the hell are you?' Joel demanded.

'Watch your mouth, kid, he's a ranger,' Quater warned. 'Cross him an' you'll not see daylight again.'

'Oh yeah? Just you wait till Lu comes

149

back. He'll make buzzard-meat outa him.'

Hardened as he was. Brad could scarely conceal his disgust at the kid's attitude. Without another word he closed the cell door with a bang and turned the key.

'That boy sure does get under my skin,' Bannerman said, echoing Brad's thoughts, as they returned along the corridor.

Doc Ryan was examining the wound in Logan's shoulder when they entered the outer office.

'Looks like we got Grimes' kid brother back there,' Brad said.

'D'you reckon his brothers'll try to spring him out?' Logan asked anxiously.

'Well, iffen they do, it ain't gonna be botherin' you,' Doc Ryan drawled. He tapped Logan's shoulder lightly. 'I gotta get a slug outa here. After that I'm prescribing rest and lots of it unless you've gotten tired of livin'.'

'I gotta meet with your father,' Brad said to Abigail. 'He'll be needin' to file an official report for his insurance claim. How do I find him?'

'He owns a spread about four hours ride out of town,' Abigail said. 'Don't worry about the damage to the bank, Ranger Saunders — my father is a reasonable man. If you're goin' that way I'd be obliged if I could go along. I'll feel a whole lot safer out there than here in town.'

* * *

'So what the hell went wrong?'

Solomon's face was purple with rage as he faced Tute and Grimes across the desk in his office in Kell.

'They was expectin' us,' Grimes growled.

His creased head was feeling sore as hell and his mood matched it.

'I guess that's so,' Tute remarked, his face impassive.

'So?' Grimes eyed Tute. 'You said you'd back me; where the hell were you?'

'I lost two men,' Tute replied. 'You got away, didn't you?'

'No thanks to you, you sonofabitch. I'm mad as hell we lost young Joel.' He shifted uncomfortably. 'Fact is, we don't know whether he's alive or dead.'

'Serves you right fer takin' him along,' Tute said.

Grimes backed off, his hand hovering over his gun. 'Shut your big mouth,' he snarled.

'You wanna make something of this?' Tute jeered, his hands poised like talons over his own weapons.

'Anytime,' Grimes snarled. 'Right now's as good as any.'

As Grimes and Tute eyed each other like dogs spoiling for a fight, Solomon moved first; his pearl-handled Colts rapidly appeared in both his hands.

'That's enough!' he shouted, pointing a weapon at each of the two men. 'Now quit arguin', we ain't got time for that.'

The tension in the room slowly eased.

'Glad you guys see sense,' Solomon

said. 'I got more'n enough on my mind since Bannerman walked out on me.'

Grimes snapped his fingers. 'It was him who was holed up in the bank along with that ranger.'

Solomon downed a glass of whiskey and poured another, pointedly ignoring his henchmen.

'Bannerman? You sure about that?'

'Bannerman!' Tute echoed. 'How the hell could it be him?'

'Well he ain't at the ranch,' Grimes said.

Solomon's expression became sullen. 'I guess I owe you guys an explanation. One of the servants told me she'd seen Abigail eavesdroppin' our last meeting. Later that night she swears she saw her leavin' the ranch with Bannerman.'

'So your wife's finally gone off with him,' Grimes said with a sly grin.

Solomon was so angry he couldn't speak.

'You sure it was Bannerman in the bank?' Tute asked. 'I never saw him pack a gun as I recall.'

'He didn't,' Grimes said. 'But I'm tellin' you, both those guys could use one — and Bannerman was one of 'em fer sure.'

Solomon opened the drawer, took out the dodger and passed it to Grimes. Tute moved in to read it over his shoulder.

'Bannerman shot Jerry Quinn?' Grimes exclaimed. 'Why Jerry had one of the fastest draws I ever saw.'

'This guy is definitely Bannerman,' Solomon said, tapping the dodger with his finger. 'When I faced him with it, he didn't deny it.'

'Then how come he's teamed up with a ranger?' Tute snapped his fingers. 'Say, is he some kinda plant? I heard McNelly ain't above doin' that kinda thing. Remember how he used Buck Duane to bust Cheseldine's gang?'

'There's only one way to find out,' Solomon said. 'Go back to Dolores an' take the place apart.'

'You're jokin'!' Grimes exclaimed.

'Why not? They won't be expecting

anything to happen for a few days.'

'We need more men,' Tute said.

'You got 'em,' Solomon snapped. 'Every man-jack on my pay-roll.'

'That'll be around fifty,' Tute said with such speed it was clear he'd done his homework.

'Somethin' like that,' Solomon agreed. 'If we don't take over Dolores now, we'll never do it.'

'You ridin' with us?' Grimes asked.

Solomon shook his head. 'I'm gonna take a dozen men and pay Eli Greensbee a visit at his ranch. I gotta score to settle there, I reckon. I'll meet you guys outside the bank in Dolores at noon the day after tomorrow.'

★　★　★

The sky was gilded like a banner with fiery tinges of red and gold heralding sunset when Brad and Abigail approached her father's ranch. As they passed by a small herd of cattle round a water-hole, Brad's keen eye took in

155

Eli Greensbee's brand-mark — an A inside a Diamond, which read correctly, from outside to inside, translated to 'Diamond A'.

A dog made a sudden rush at them out of a thicket and began to bark furiously.

'Halt. Who goes there?'

Brad reined Blaze in at the time-honoured command from the puncher delegated to sentry-go, aware of the Winchester pointing at him.

'Oh, it's you, Miss Abigail.'

The puncher dropped his Winchester from high port and stooped to silence the dog.

'Say, ma'am, it's real good to see you. I'm real sorry I didn't recognize you, but I guess I ain't seen you in a long time.'

'Don't you worry none, Luke,' Abigail replied. She dismounted and drew her horse after her. 'I'm glad you're keepin' watch.'

'I guess your pa's taking precautions, Miss Abigail. They reckon things is gettin' bad along the county line. No-one's saying who's behind it, but we got a good idea.' Luke looked embarrassed as he spoke.

'Well you needn't worry on my account,' Abigail said with a light laugh. 'This man is Sergeant Saunders of the Texas Rangers.'

'Lordy, lordy! Iffen the rangers is here, there must be somethin' amiss. An' a full-blown sergeant, too! But I guess you'll be wantin' a word with your pappy.'

'How is he, Luke?'

The man made a wry face. 'He's fine, I guess. Gimme your hosses, I'll take good care of 'em for you.' He gave a loud whistle which brought a man to the door of the barn. 'Hey, Lofty, gimme a hand, will you?'

Brad removed his hat and dusted himself down before he followed Abigail onto the stoop. The door opened as they appoached and a coloured maid met them.

'Sarah!' Abigail exclaimed.

'Oh Missy Abigail, my baby! You've come home at last!'

Brad stood clear as Abigail became engulfed in the woman's fulsome embrace.

'Can I see my father?' Abigail asked.

'Of course you can. Oh Missy, you don't know how full of sorrow he been. Every night I've prayed to the Lord this day would come.'

Eli Greensbee was a wealthy man and it showed. The ranch-house was built in hacienda style and once inside Brad's boots sank into a thick-piled carpet running along a corridor lined with old guns, hunting-trophies and oil-paintings as he followed Abigail and Sarah to her father's study.

Sarah knocked and waited.

'Come in,' a deep voice boomed.

Sarah opened the door and ushered Abigail and Brad into the smoke-filled inner sanctum.

Eli Greensbee's vast bulk occupied a huge leather-bound chair behind an oak desk cluttered with papers. His full beard and great mane of hair, both as white as snow, gave him the appearance of an Old Testament prophet. The blue haze of smoke from his curved pipe swirling in the yellow lamplight partly obscured the lines of books behind the glass-fronted shelves which ran from the floor to the ceiling behind him.

But what caught Brad's eye and held it was the portrait in oils hanging on one wall. The painter had captured the fine bone structure of the woman's face with remarkable clarity. Several moments elapsed before he realized it was Abigail . . .

'So you've finally come home, child.' Eli Greensbee's basso profondo voice, speaking slowly and with precision, trembled with emotion as he laid his pipe to one side.

'I was wrong,' Abigail said, tears streaming down her face. 'Will you ever forgive me? Oh Daddy!'

For answer, Eli Greensbee rose from his chair and held out his arms. No more words were spoken but Brad knew he was privileged to witness the rebirth of a shattered relationship.

'And now you must introduce me to the man who has brought you here,' Eli Greensbee said.

He listened in silence as Abigail explained what had happened and Brad gave his account of the raid on the bank.

'So Earl Solomon has finally run amok,' Eli Greensbee said when he had finished. 'Just as I predicted. *As ye sow, so shall ye reap*. But I am forgetting myself . . .'

He rose to pour a glass of fine claret for Abigail and whiskey for himself and Brad.

'Thank you for escorting my daughter back home, Sergeant Saunders. Thank God none of my employees at the bank was killed or injured. I have you to thank for that. I understand your disappointment, but I applaud your attempt to apprehend the robbers. What do you propose to do next?'

'Make out an insurance report for

you, sir, and then return to Dolores in the morning.'

'And what do you think Earl Solomon's next move will be?'

'He has a lot of badmen on his pay-roll,' Abigail said. 'Earl got rid of all the decent hands Frank set on.'

'I suspect he can raise a sizeable force,' Eli Greensbee observed. 'Do you think he might be bold enough to try to take over Dolores?'

'He will if he thinks I'm there,' Abigail said.

Eli Greensbee cocked his eye at Brad.

'Well, I reckon after he's chewed the fat over with Tute and Grimes, he might just do that,' Brad said.

'You're going to need help,' Eli Greensbee said. 'I take it Captain McNelly isn't available?'

Brad shook his head. 'He's a sick man. When I saw him he was talkin' 'bout being replaced.'

Eli Greensbee stroked his beard thoughtfully.

'I'm sorry to hear that. McNelly's

done a fine job, I only hope his successor is worthy of him. Look, Sergeant Saunders, I've twenty men at my disposal.' He gave a wry smile. 'Some of them have had the odd brush with the law, but the Good Lord has convinced them of the error of their ways. They're a loyal bunch, even if it's only because I pay them well and don't ask a lot of fool questions about their past. I'm not a Calvinist, I don't believe in hell-fire and damnation for all except the favoured few. Redemption is open to every man who puts his trust in the Lord. They are at your disposal whenever you wish.'

'That's mighty generous of you, Mr Greensbee,' Brad said.

'Good, that's settled then. And Now I suppose you're both ready to eat?'

* * *

Grimes left Solomon's office and tramped along the sidewalk to Micah's saloon. His brothers, including the chastened Frank, were waiting for him at the bar. The latter eyed him warily, but Grimes had other things on his mind.

'Solomon's just told Tute to raise an army an' take over Dolores,' he said.

'So you've been demoted?' Zeke said. He gave a grimace. 'You mean to say I got this sore ass fer nuthin'?'

He poured a whiskey and slid it across the bar. Grimes picked it up and downed it.

'You might just say that,' he agreed.

'What about the kid?' Frank asked. He drew heavily on a cigar as he spoke.

His brothers murmured assent.

'We gotta find out what's happened to him,' Curt said.

'You think I don't figure that?' Grimes said. 'It's been on my mind ever since he went missin'.'

'I reckon we should get in there ahead of Tute,' Zeke said.

'If we go steamin' in again, we'll be stickin' our necks in a noose fer sure,' Jud pointed out.

'I wasn't with you,' Frank said. 'Nobody will know who I am. Supposin' I ride in and take a look-see?'

Zeke spat neatly into a spittoon. 'You sure you're feelin' up to it, Frank?' he demanded. There was no humour in his voice as he spoke.

'I'll live,' Frank replied, easing his crotch uncomfortably.

'I don't reckon there's any other way,' Curt said.

'OK,' Grimes snapped. 'Me an' the boys'll ride with you. We'll hole up just outside town an' wait until we hear from you.'

*　★　★

As Brad rode into Main Street, Dolores, a shirt-sleeved barkeep emerged through the batwings of a saloon and despite the handicap of a wooden leg, hobbled along the sidewalk as fast as the other and a crutch would carry him.

Brad reined in alongside him.

'Somethin' happening, mister?' he asked.

In his haste, the man didn't recognize Brad. 'You bet,' he retorted. 'You'd better shift yore ass, mister, otherwise you're gonna miss a mighty fine hangin'.'

Brad's lantern jaw hardened. Even as he eased Blaze forward, a great roar filled the air, making the big bay stallion whicker uneasily. The fine hairs in the nape of Brad's neck stood on end. This was the primeval roar of a crowd baying for blood; it carried the same spine-chilling timbre he'd once heard at a bullfight.

As he cantered along, he passed a long line of empty stores and saloons, their doors swinging idly in the warm breeze. When he came to the livery stable, the crowd had swollen to the proportions of a Mexican fiesta, spilling off the raised sidewalks into the dusty street. Cowhands, gamblers, shopkeepers, clerks, saloon-girls, good women, even children — it seemed like all the world was heading towards the town centre.

Brad dismounted outside the livery stable but could find no-one to receive Blaze, so he tethered the stallion alongside half a dozen others on the shady side of the street and set off to walk the last hundred yards on foot.

As he drew closer he became increasingly aware of the hostility in the faces of the people jostling around him. Closer in, he observed that their attention was focused on a line of trees affording shade to the sidewalk.

'I say let's give him the rope!' A stentorian voice rose above the crowd which responded with a roar of approval.

As Brad thrust his way forward a rope snaked over one of the branches of the tallest tree. There was a scuffle to his left and several men appeared from Logan's office.

Brad jabbed his elbow viciously into the ribs of a bulking teamster in his haste to break through the mob. He sensed the age-old alchemy of fear, hatred and anarchy in the air. A mob

166

baying for blood. His mouth tightened to a hyphen. What in the world was Logan doing allowing a prisoner to be taken out of his custody and lynched?

His question was soon answered, for as he forced his way through the mob Cally appeared in the doorway, her face distraught. Bannerman was alongside her, his right arm in a sling.

'I'm warnin' you!' Bannerman bawled. 'There'll be hell to pay if you go through with this.'

'Who from?' a heavily-built man in shirt-sleeves and wearing a blood-stained butcher's apron shouted. 'Not from the ranger, that's fer sure. He's left town. He's had a bellyful. I bet we never see him again. C'mon boys, what are we waitin' for? Let's string him up.'

The roar of the crowd engulfed his words. Scuffles began again as several men pounced and began to haul the struggling prisoner towards the make-shift gallows.

As he passed by, Brad saw the bitterly defiant expression on Joel's face. A trickle of blood ran down his jaw from where he had lost a tooth. With difficulty, Brad swallowed the bile rising in his mouth.

'Murderer!'

'Hang him!'

Joel snarling defiance at his captors, struggled every inch of the way as they dragged him through the crowd. His resistance lashed the crowd into fury and when the first gobbet of spit splashed into his face from a respectably dressed woman, Brad went into action.

Using his fists and elbows without stinting, Brad fought his way through to the sidewalk. By the time he had emerged at Cally's side, the mob had manhandled their victim to a barebacked horse and were about to drop a noose round his neck.

'Fer God's sake, will you not see reason?'

Cally's anguished plea was lost in the chorus of angry shouts. A pack of dogs howled a shrill descant to the braying of an ass and the neighing of tethered horses as the animals caught the scent of rage and fear sweeping through the crowd.

'They won't listen! Oh God, what can we do?'

Cally wrung her hands in anguish as she spoke. Overcoming her terror with a visible effort, she cried, 'Can't you see, he's only a boy?'

'He ain't no boy, he's one of that murderin' gang of bank-robbers!' a florid-faced man dressed in a smart grey suit shouted.

When the patience of the town's solid citizens had snapped, Brad knew something had gone badly wrong.

Joel was mounted roughly astride the unsaddled horse and his hands secured behind his back. The noose was dropped round his neck. It was the moment of truth, as the Mexicans called it — that microcosm of time before the matador glides his rapier between the eyes of a bull and kills it.

Thirty paces away, high on the

sidewalk, Brad drew his Peacemaker and, bracing it across his forearm, he took careful aim. He pulled the trigger a fraction of a second before the man who had drawn his hat could slap it across the rump of the horse. The gun spat a yellow tongue of flame and the man froze like a waxwork with his arm aloft as the bullet whined within an inch of his head.

'Hold it!' Brad's harsh voice cut the air with the ferocity of a whiplash. His command imposed utter silence on the crowd.

The man holding the head of the horse brought the bucking animal under control. The other, holding the Stetson, unwound slowly from his backswing and turned to stare malevolently at Brad.

'Who the hell are you?'

A low murmur rippled through the crowd.

'Glory be, it's the ranger!' a voice exclaimed.

Brad stepped forward, the muzzle of

his Colt still wisping smoke. Mindful of Captain McNelly's advice, he realized that now was not the time to play the hero. It was clear that law and order had broken down. As an excited babble of conversation broke out, he held up his hand for silence.

'I've just arrived back in town,' he said. 'An' I find this.'

He glowered across at the prisoner. Joel was still sitting astride the horse, his hands roped behind his back and the noose still round his neck. The expression on his face was a mixture of relief and defiance.

'An' it seems like I wasn't a moment too soon,' Brad went on. 'If you'd gone through with this business, there'd have been a helluva lot of explainin' to do.'

Already he sensed that his reasonable tone was shaming the more even-handed citizens into seeing the folly of their behaviour. He reinforced his faith in their influence by holstering his gun.

'He was caught red-handed,' a man said sullenly. 'This here young feller was holding the horses, while the rest of his gang tried to rob the bank.'

Brad held up his hand for silence. 'You think I don't know that? Now see here, folks. What kind of a town is it that could lynch a young boy?' He looked round, visibly shocked. 'Why, I can see women and children here among you.'

'He's right. What right have any of you to take the law into your own hands?'

It was Cally who spoke. She faced the crowd, hands on hips, her face white with anger. 'Will you not listen to Sergeant Saunders?'

The citizens on the fringe of the crowd were already beginning to disperse when Brad snapped, 'OK, folks, the show's over.' He turned to Bannerman. 'Put the boy back in the cells.' Then he followed Cally back into the office.

'What sparked that off?' he demanded.

Cally turned her back to him.

'Well?' Brad asked.

Suddenly it dawned on him that she was crying.

He stepped forward and put his hands gently on her shoulders.

'Why, Cally, what's wrong?'

As she turned her distraught face towards him, he felt sick to the bottom of his soul.

'Pa's dead,' she said slowly. 'That's what's caused all this trouble. I found him in bed this morning. Doc Ryan said he'd had heart failure. The operation to get the bullet out of his shoulder was too much for him. Oh, Brad, what am I gonna do?'

Before he could reply, Bannerman's voice called out urgently from the doorway, 'Hey, Brad, there's a bunch of guys headin' this way. They look real mean . . . '

8

Brad drew his Peacemaker, Bannerman snatched up a Winchester and they ran for the door. But it was too late, the men had already dismounted and one of them was already striding towards them.

'Who the hell are they? Bannerman muttered, screwing his eyes against the sun.

'Solomon's men?' Brad suggested.

'Hold your fire, sergeant!' one of the men called out amidst a shout of laughter.

Brad's jaw dropped in amazement. Suddenly his face cracked into a broad smile.

'Why it's Jim Miller, as I live an' breathe!' he exclaimed.

'Brad! You old sonofagun!'

Brad holstered his gun and went forward to greet his oldest ranger friend.

'I take it you are Sergeant Saunders?'

The leading rider dismounted, hitched his horse and walked over to Brad.

'Name's Lee Hall, I'm your new lieutenant,' the man said, extending his hand. 'You seemed a mite edgy just now, sergeant. Everything under control?'

Brad nodded as they shook hands. 'I guess so.'

Hall smiled reassuringly. 'You took a big job on here, even for a man with your reputation. Back in San Antonio, Captain McNelly dropped me a strong hint you might need some help so I brought a dozen men along. Like to fill me in with what's been happening?'

Lieutenant Hall was a tall man. Inasmuch as he wore a moustache and was dressed in a casual shirt, vest and pants he looked exactly like his fellow rangers, but he exuded an air of authority which set him apart. As soon as he saw Cally he removed his Stetson, revealing the flame-coloured hair which had already earned him the sobriquet

175

'Red' amongst the men of the Special Company.

He listened carefully while Brad explained the situation.

'So you think Solomon's men will come back?' he said when Brad had finished.

'I reckon so, sir,' Brad replied. 'It's my belief — and Mr Bannerman here agrees — that Solomon is tryin' to gain control of Vance County.'

'Extendin' his kingdom, huh? How many men can he count on?'

Brad looked at Bannerman.

'He has the Grimes brothers and Tute's men. They are the gunmen,' Bannerman said. 'But then there's his ranch-hands, the guys who work at the factory and any other riff-raff who'll go along for the ride. One way or another I reckon he can field upwards of fifty men.'

Red Hall whistled. 'Say, that's quite an army.'

'Hadn't we better start organizing our defences, sir?' Brad said. 'Sheriff

Logan only had time to deputize a few men.'

Red Hall smiled. 'No, sergeant, as soon as the horses have rested, we're movin' out.'

Brad was aghast.

'But with respect, sir, we can't pull out and leave Dolores undefended . . . '

'Sergeant Saunders, as far as I'm concerned, Dolores isn't in danger,' Hall snapped. 'We're ridin' into Kell. How long is that gonna take?' he demanded of Bannerman.

'Around six hours if you don't want to blow your horses. But wait a minute, surely you ain't gonna ride into Solomon's kingdom with only a handful of men!'

'Mr Bannerman, each and every one of my men is worth ten outlaws,' Hall said brusquely. 'If Solomon could field a hundred, it wouldn't worry me. Now, Sergeant Saunders, I'm hungry. Surely in your brief stay here you must have found some place to eat?'

'Aint no need for you to do that,'

Cally said. 'I can cook for you and Brad — and Mr Bannerman, too, if he's so minded.'

Brad shifted uncomfortably as he saw the amused glint in Hall's eyes.

'Cally, we don't want to put you to no trouble, seeing as what just happened,' Brad said awkwardly.

'It ain't no problem,' Cally replied stoutly. 'Pa may be dead but we're still here and we gotta keep our strength up.'

★　★　★

Inside the cell, Joel was sitting on the bench, his face as glum as an undertaker's mute. Alongside him a solitary fly circled over a plate which once had contained a portion of beans.

'What's the matter, kid? We finished your chuck 'cos we never thought you was comin' back. Ain't you glad you're still alive?' It was Pete Moses who spoke.

'Hell, I thought it was the drop fer all of us when that lot came bustin' in,' Al

Quater said. He was standing on tiptoe peering out of the tiny barred window which admitted the only daylight into the cell.

'I thought Lu would be here by now,' Joel said dismally.

'You reckon he's gonna risk his hide to spring you out?' Moses showed an incomplete set of foul yellow stumps as he brayed his version of a laugh.

'He will, he's my brother.'

'He surely won't, not now this bunch has ridden into town,' Quater said.

'Whaddya mean?' The youngster looked up in alarm.

'Step over here, junior, an' take a look.'

Joel joined Quater by the window.

'If they ain't rangers I'm a Dutchman,' Quater growled.

'How can you tell?'

'Dunno — I just know, that's all. Look, see, that ranger who arrested us, he's talkin' real respectful with that big red-haired guy who rode in at the head of 'em.'

'Hell, what are we gonna do, Al?'

The first sign of desperation appeared in the youngster's face as he spoke.

'Hey, look!'

Man and boy by the window turned to look at Moses who was on his hands and knees beside the outer wall.

'What in the world are you doin', Pete?' Quater said irritably. 'You sure do get on a man's nerves . . . '

'Look, see here!' Moses said excitedly. He was scrabbling away at the base of the wall with a spoon handle.

'Oh come on, Pete, fer God's sake give us a break,' Quater said.

Pete took no notice. He jiggled and scraped away at the crumbling mortar between the crudely laid stones. When one of them moved slightly, his two companions joined him.

Pete leaned back and wiped the sweat from his forehead and grinned.

'Boys, very soon one good kick's gonna bring this lot down like a house of cards,' he said. 'Iffen we play the joker right, we could be outa here sooner than you think . . . '

        ★   ★   ★

Outside the town, Grimes and his brothers were playing monte in an abandoned Mexican *jacal* when Frank burst in on them, rain streaming in rivulets from his faded yellow oilskin slicker.

'The kid's alive!' he announced.

Grimes leapt to his feet, overturning the table, scattering cards and coins onto the floor.

'Alive, you say? Where is he?'

Frank divested himself of the dripping slicker and flung it into a corner. 'He's in the jail. Just after I arrived word went round the sheriff had croaked. The citizens blew up a head of steam and the kid was damn near lynched. Wasn't nothin' I could do about it. But the kid was lucky. The ranger had been outa town. He rode in in the nick of time and saved him.'

'What are we gonna do now?' Curt exclaimed.

Frank mopped his brow with his bandanna. He picked up a half-full bottle of beer and drained it.

'That ain't all,' he said, wiping his lips with the back of his hand. 'He ain't the only one. The whole place is crawlin' with 'em. Half an hour later a big red-haired guy rode in at the head of a whole company.'

'Jesus, they'll be McNelly's men.' Zeke swore loud and long. He eased himself carefully to his feet, for his bullet-creased backside was as sore as hell. 'That's all we needed.'

'Looks like we got no chance of freein' the kid,' Curt agreed. His head was bound with a dirty white bandage covering the crease he'd taken during the assault on the bank.

'I reckon we have,' Frank said quietly. 'I decided to hang around a bit longer. The rangers rode outa town about an hour ago — every man-jack of 'em, includin' the sergeant.'

'They've pulled out? I don't believe it!' Zeke exclaimed. 'Where were they headin'?'

'You know what I reckon?' Frank said. 'I reckon they're gonna hit Kell before Tute and his men come here.'

'You what?' Grimes roared, his face a mask of disbelief.

'If they get there before daylight they'll take 'em by surprise,' Zeke said. 'A guy caught with his pants down ain't much use in a fight.'

The room fell silent.

'There's more.' Frank continued as he fashioned a smoke. 'It was definitely Bannerman who helped the ranger at the bank. Logan deputized him and the rangers have left him in charge while they're gone. But he's got one arm in a sling — a fella I was drinkin' with told me he took a nasty one during the raid . . . '

'Bannerman's in charge?' Grimes grinned as he clapped Frank on the shoulder. 'Frank, you done a great job. Why, I take back all them things I said about you earlier. Boys, I reckon we got a great chance to snatch the kid outa that jail. After that, I reckon it's time we parted company with Solomon.'

'You mean we're pullin' out?' Curt said with raised eyebrows.

Grimes nodded. 'There's no future here. If we move out now, by the time the rangers have finished with Solomon and Tute we'll be long gone.'

'Ed, I reckon that's real smart thinkin',' Jud remarked.

'One of us has to do some,' Grimes said sarcastically.

'Maybe we should finish the job off at the bank while we're about it?' Frank said. 'I sure could use some cash . . . '

'So you can get the clap again? You gotta be jokin',' Grimes said sourly. 'Now let's get goin' . . . '

* * *

It was late afternoon when Lieutenant Red Hall led his rangers out of Dolores on the dusty trail that led to Kell. To the south a heavy bank of grey cloud presaged the rain so badly needed by the arid landscape.

As they rode out of Dolores, to the casual observer, they looked a clean-cut bunch of *hombres*, some old enough to sport full moustaches twirled upwards to finely-pointed tips, others so young their faces hardly needed a scratch with a razor. But they had one thing in common — they were all hand-picked by McNelly, and what impressed Brad was that despite the fact they had only known their new leader for a week or so they accepted him as such without question.

'That was a real fine meal Cally Logan cooked for us back there,' Lee Hall remarked to Brad as they cantered along. 'Say, d'you reckon she's taken a shine for Lee Bannerman?'

'What's the plan, sir?' Brad asked, swiftly changing the subject.

'Well, I propose we ride through the night and hit Kell in the early hours;

I'm playing this low-key. We ain't goin' in with all guns blazing; we're the law, not an invadin' army. We'll slip into town quietly with the object of locating and arresting the leaders. We know the layout from what Bannerman's told us, so we'll divide into two groups and work along both sides of the main street concentrating on the lodging-houses. If we work quietly and without fuss we should soon locate the whereabouts of Solomon, Tute and Grimes. Once we've arrested them, I don't anticipate any further resistance. We can't handle large numbers of prisoners, but my theory is that without leaders the rank and file will lose heart. What do you think?'

Brad nodded. The plan was simple, but sound, conceived by a man who knew what he was about.

As the first heavy drops of rain began to fall, Hall called a halt to allow his men to don their *serapes*, a garment highly thought of by the members of the Special Company and a concession to Mexican superiority over the usual slickers sold in stores all over the West.

A multi-pronged fork of lightning seared the darkening sky. It was followed by a long, low drum-roll of thunder and without further warning the rain came tumbling down like a waterfall.

It was going to be a long, wet ride . . .

★   ★   ★

Earl Solomon reined in at the head of his men, pausing to gaze at the Diamond A ranch-house on the distant horizon.

'We goin' straight in, boss?'

It was Noah Cropper who spoke. He was as blond as a Viking and his face glowed as red when it was exposed to the heat of the sun. He minimized this effect by wearing his Stetson so low it all but concealed the upper part of his face.

Solomon's white teeth gleamed as his lips drew back in a dazzling smile.

'Sure, why not?' He rose in his saddle

to address the dozen men he had with him. 'Whatever happens, I want the old man and my wife unharmed, ya hear?'

There was a murmur of assent, followed by a pause while Solomon lighted a Havana cigar.

'OK, let's go.'

With a chorus of spine-chilling rebel whoops and shrieks, Solomon and his men descended on the unsuspecting inhabitants of the Diamond A.

The guard appeared, only to be shot down in cold blood along with his dog by the still smiling Solomon. Within five minutes, his men had either killed, dispersed or rounded up and disarmed any hands who were about.

In the midst of the chaos, the tall patrician figure of Eli Greensbee appeared in the doorway. He was unarmed but the old man's presence was sufficient to bring the mayhem to a stop. Solomon and his men froze like a bunch of schoolboys caught misbehaving by their headmaster.

But Solomon soon recovered from

his father-in-law's disconcerting presence.

'Well, now Eli, I guess I just stopped by to pay my respects.'

Eli Greensbee eyed his son-in-law coldly. 'You have a strange way of doing it.'

'I'm not coming back, Earl, not ever!' Solomon's expression changed as Abigail slipped past her father and faced him.

'I think that's somethin' we're gonna have to talk about,' Solomon replied ominously as he dismounted.

As he tossed his bridle to one of the Diamond A hands, the menace in his voice intimidated Abigail who shrank back to the safety of her father's arm.

'My daughter has intimated to me that she does not wish to have anything further to do with you,' Eli Greensbee said quietly.

'Oh, yeah?' Solomon sneered. A cold glitter entered his eyes. 'She happens to be my wife, just in case you'd forgotten.'

'From what she has told me, you have forfeited any right to be called her husband,' the old man replied. 'In fact I have always suspected that you were responsible for her first husband's death.'

Solomon drew one of his guns faster than a magician palming a card.

'No!' Abigail screamed as she dashed forward to interpose herself between her husband and her father.

Solomon flung her aside brutally and took a step forward. For a few seconds the atmosphere in the yard was as silent and menacing as a spinney over which a hawk hovers.

'I could kill you for that, Eli, but I won't.' Solomon's shrill high voice pierced the stillness. 'The other day my men failed to rob your bank. When we ride into town tomorrow, you're gonna open that safe for me.' He looked down at Abigail who was staring at him white-faced. 'Iffen you don't, I promise you'll be burying your daughter . . . '

Like most towns, Dolores fell silent from around two in the morning until dawn. By this time even the most dedicated gambler or liquor-sodden reprobate had finally yielded to the temporary respite of sleep before the next bout of debauchery.

It was about this time that the three inhabitants of the cell inside the jail became very active indeed. Joel Grimes watched the efforts of his companions to release another brick in the outer wall with a dubious expression on his face.

'Supposin' we do get out, what we gonna do then?' he asked.

'Aw kid, fer Gawd's sake,' Al Quater pleaded. 'Stop bleatin' and give us a hand.'

He heaved and pulled until another brick came away. At that moment, the cell was illuminated by a vivid flash of lightning followed by a clap of thunder that made the whole building quiver.

'Hell, it's pissin' down,' Pete Moses said disgustedly.

'So what?' Quater said, 'There ain't gonna be a cat out in this lot. Now come on.'

Joel bent to join the two men as they redoubled their efforts, scrabbling away with their bare hands at the next layer of loosened stone . . .

★   ★   ★

On the first clap of thunder, Grimes and his brothers entered the town. As the first heavy drops of rain fell they paused to put on their slickers.

As they rode down the deserted Main Street, the flickers of lightning and rolls of thunder made their horses skittish, but Grimes's face was hard and unrelenting. They stopped outside the sheriff's office and dismounted. The twins held the horses while Grimes, Zeke and Frank walked up to the office door.

It was locked, Grimes took out his

gun and hammered hard with the butt.

'Who is it?' Bannerman's voice called from within.

'I'm one of McNelly's rangers. I got news for you. Open up!' Zeke bellowed.

The bolts drew and as Bannerman opened the door the three brothers piled in overwhelming him in the rush.

'Rope him up,' Grimes ordered the other two. 'Now where's the cell key?'

When Bannerman didn't reply, Grimes raised his gun and cocked it and pointed it at Bannerman's elbow.

'One bullet here means you lose this arm for keeps. That's just fer starters. Nothing would give me more pleasure than to shoot chunks offen you. You savvy, Bannerman?'

'It's in the drawer yonder,' came the reply.

Grimes moved across to the desk, opened the centre drawer, produced the key and held it up. When Bannerman nodded he walked across to the door which led to the cells followed by his brothers.

As they opened the door the storm reached its height. Grimes stepped forward, key in hand, fumbling for the lock, trying to see with night vision completely destroyed by a wicked blue flash of fork lightning. As he flung open the door a teeth-jarring clap of thunder coincided with another mighty crash, a chorus of surprised yells and suddenly the damp air was full of choking dust.

Grimes blundered forward into the cell, his bearings gone completely. All he could hear were muffled shouts and curses. Ahead of him where he was sure there should be a wall he found nothing and suddenly to his intense surprise, as he dove forward, hampered by his slicker, he found himself outside in the street in the pouring rain.

'What the hell is going on?' he roared in between two massive thunderclaps.

Shadowy figures scrambled towards him over a pile of rubble.

'Lu! It's me, Joel!'

Moments later they re-entered the

jail. Joel paused to help himself to Bannerman's guns and raced outside to join his brothers and the two escaped outlaws.

'What the hell happened in there?' Curt asked.

'We was trying to break out when the whole wall collapsed,' Joel told him excitedly. 'Man, you should have seen it!'

The thunder had attenuated to a mutter and the lightning flashes mere flickers by the time the outlaws were reassembled. The storm had been of sufficient intensity to screen the break-out entirely and Grimes was cock-a-hoop as he remounted his horse.

'OK, boys, we'll go get you some horses,' he said to the erstwhile prisoners.

A few minutes later, the startled owner of a nearby livery barn awoke to find himself surrounded by a circle of uncompromising faces. Once they were saddled up, Quater and Moses walked across to where Grimes was waiting.

'You ready to ride, boys?' Grimes asked affably as he stubbed out a cigarette.

'Sure,' Moses said respectfully. 'We're mighty glad you came along but, well, I guess with that wall falling down the way it did, we'd've gotten free anyways.'

Grimes nodded. 'I'm obliged to you fer takin' care of the kid,' he said.

'Which way are you plannin' on goin'?' Moses asked.

'North, I reckon.' Grimes grinned to himself.

'What about Solomon?' Quater asked him.

Grimes hawked and spat. 'He's finished. There's a whole company of rangers ridden to Kell earlier this evening.'

Moses exchanged glances with Quater. 'Maybe we oughta ride back to Kell and see.'

Grimes shoved a foot in his stirrup and mounted his horse. 'Suit yourselves,' he said.

They left the town behind them and

came to a fork in the trail.

'We'll part company here, I guess. We're obliged to you, Grimes,' Moses said politely, tipping his Stetson.

'Guess you are,' Grimes replied.

The Grimes brothers crowded their horses alongside their eldest brother.

'*Adios.*'

'*Adios,*' Grimes said.

As Quater and Moses turned to take the road to Kell, Grimes drew his gun and shot each of them through the back.

As the dead outlaws slumped forward in their saddles, young Joel spurred his horse forward.

'What the hell did you do that for, Lu?' he shouted, his face twisted in anguish. 'Those guys helped me escape.'

'Lesson number one, kid,' Grimes growled. 'Never tell anyone where you're headin'.'

9

At last the seemingly interminable trail to Kell was coming to an end. The night was black as pitch and the rain was still falling in torrents but the rangers contrived to light a fire under the shelter of an overhanging rock and make some java — a brew so strong that it would float iron and eat holes in the pot if left to stand.

Looking round him, Brad felt a warm glow of reassurance as he returned the smiles and banter of comrades he knew he could rely on totally. It reminded him of the fellowship of his company during the war ... of Captain Walt Dawson and other men long since dead, but whose faces still flickered in the flames of every camp-fire when he travelled alone. The memory of such men was what drove Brad on; it fuelled the urge to justify his own survival and to strain every nerve to build the kind of world such men had hoped for.

'OK, boys, let's go,' Hall said. The fire sizzled and spat as the men flung the dregs from their mugs onto the flames. The sound of creaking of leather filled the air as the men saddled their horses and tightened the double cinches ready for the final canter into Kell.

Half an hour later, their eyes, accustomed to the dark, could just pick out the finger-like profile of the chimney-stack of the factory. Although the rain was still falling, the dampness failed to relieve the smell of decay which pervaded the atmosphere.

As they approached the first cluster of *jacals* on the outskirts Brad observed that Kell was much smaller than Dolores. The weather was so foul that as the horses splashed along the heavily-rutted road into the sleeping town, not even a cat ventured forth to observe their passing.

Hall signalled his men to stop outside

a livery stable not far from the town centre.

'I want these animals fed and watered immediately,' he ordered the goggle-eyed, gap-toothed old-timer who peered round the door.

'Who the hell are you?' the old-timer demanded.

'Lieutenant Hall, Texas Rangers. I'm here on business, so I'd be obliged if you'd not shout it from the rooftops.'

'Yessir!' the old-timer exclaimed as he stooped to catch the coin Hall flipped at him.

'Where can we find Solomon?' Hall demanded.

The old-timer shook his head. 'Mr Solomon ain't here in town, that's fer sure. His horse would be stabled here iffen he was.'

'Jordan Tute?'

The old-timer sniggered as he pointed a bony finger. 'He's over yonder at Clementine's.'

'Grimes?'

'I guess Lucifer's around someplace.

He usually leaves his horses at Drogan's Livery near the factory.' The old-timer hawked and spat. 'I guess he ain't as partic'lar as Tute.'

Hall had already divided his men, taking half himself and allocating the other half to Brad. His final briefing over the coffee-break had been a model of clarity.

'OK, boys, let's get this over with.'

His demeanour was as calm as a deacon speaking in a church.

'Sergeant Saunders, you will arrest Tute. I'll take yonder lodging-house on the right. I want no noise, mind. Deal with any men who are hostile. And remember — at the end of the day I want the ringleaders alive so they can be given a fair trial.'

'He's got a different way of operating to McNelly,' Miller muttered to Brad as they hived off.

Brad shrugged. 'Things have gotta change, I reckon. McNelly did a good job, but I've heard the authorities in Austin ain't too happy with us emptying saddles before we ask questions.'

'Clementine's Place,' Miller muttered with a wry smile as he read the dripping sign above them. 'A whorehouse if ever I saw one.'

Guns drawn under *serapes*, the rangers followed Brad onto the boarded sidewalk and through the door.

Once inside, the stomach-churning stench from the abbatoir yielded to a pot-pourri of sweat, cheap perfume and stale tobacco-smoke. A raised bar with a brass foot-rail faced them; across the far side of the room a wide staircase led to a gallery containing the suite of rooms where the women entertained their clients. The bar was unoccupied save for a sleeping dog which woke and wandered quietly over to them, its tail wagging twenty to the dozen.

'Place seems friendly enough,' Miller muttered ironically as he bent to pat the dog before he followed Brad stealthily up the staircase.

'Remember, boys, quietly — the

lieutenant doesn't want no fuss,' Brad reminded them in a low voice when they arrived at the top.

'Kid gloves an' no bad language,' Miller said with a low laugh.

'What do you boys want? All my girls are busy.'

Brad turned about to face an open door filled with a woman of Junoesque proportions. Her appearance in a floor-length nightdress, wearing a night-cap and holding a candle was so incongruous that the rangers burst out laughing.

'Holy cow! You must be my darlin' Clementine,' Miller spluttered.

'I ain't jokin'!' the woman exclaimed. 'You boys had best get outa here before Jordan has your hides for the factory.'

'Speaking of whom,' Brad said, fighting to keep his face straight, 'you got any knowledge of his whereabouts?'

Clementine's eyes narrowed. 'Who's askin'?'

'Sergeant Saunders, Texas Rangers.'

The woman's mouth dropped open

so wide Brad figured it might never close again.

'Jordan!' she bawled back into the room. 'Get the hell outa here!'

Brad and Miller darted forward. Miller grunted as he collided with Clementine and came to a dead stop against her not inconsiderable buttocks. By the time Brad had fandangoed past the pair of them the lanky figure of the outlaw was disappearing out of the window, naked as the day he was born.

Brad crossed the room in three bounds and looked outside. Below him was the rickety verandah which covered the boardwalk. Tute was already sliding down a support into the road below. Brad watched in disbelief as the outlaw's white body disappeared in the pouring rain in the direction of the factory.

From behind came muffled exclamations from the surprised clients as his men methodically entered each room and surprised and disarmed them.

'Hall will skin us if we lose him,'

Miller muttered.

'Come on, what are we waitin' for?'

Brad turned round and made for the door.

The whorehouse was quiet enough for the rest of the men had now rounded up the occupants. The women were mainly of Mexican origin. The men were in various states of undress and in that condition the shrewd Red Hall had figured it was difficult for anyone to put up serious resistance, or as he had succinctly put it, 'Boys, a man is pretty useless without his pants on.'

'I'm going after Tute,' Brad said to Miller. 'Jim, you go report that to the lieutenant. The rest of you boys know what to do.'

The rangers had already piled up an impressive collection of levis. Miller bent down and began to rope them up into a crude bundle.

'What the hell are you playin' at?' Clementine shouted as Brad made to leave.

'OK, boys,' Brad said to the

assembled patrons. 'It's three o'clock an' it's wet outside. Ain't no place fer you to go except back to bed. Why waste good money after all?'

A sentiment which was received with unanimous agreement.

* * *

Tute sprinted the two hundred yards to the factory at a pace which left him panting for breath. He knew the layout well. It consisted of a long shed with a ramp at one end to the top of which the cattle were driven before they were slaughtered. The carcases were then dropped through a trap-door to the ground-floor level where they were skinned. At the opposite end were the boilers where the tallow was separated out and skimmed off into the barrels.

He stopped and glanced behind him. No-one appeared to be following him. All he needed was enough breathing-space to get some clothes, a horse and preferably a gun then he could get the hell out of this place.

His arrival at the factory disturbed a bunch of steers awaiting their fate in the corral outside. Tute tensed, ready to act, as their persistent lowing brought the elderly nightwatchman to the door of his cabin.

The man's bleary eyes widened when he saw Tute in his state of nature.

'Why, Mr Tute! What in the world . . . ' was all he got out before Tute's fist smashed into his jaw, knocking him unconscious.

Tute bent down over the inert body and hastily removed the man's vest, shirt and trousers. The man was at least six inches shorter than he was and the clothes gave him the grotesque appearance of a circus clown.

But Tute didn't have a mirror and he was past caring. At least now he felt like a man again. He picked up the watchman's gunbelt and strapped it about his waist. The weapon was a well-worn Army Colt. All he needed now was a horse from the corral at the far end of the factory. But whilst he was checking the loads in the Colt he heard a noise out in the street . . .

He opened the door and peered out. The rain was still falling heavily, bouncing off the ground, running in miniature rivers along the cart-ruts in the pitch-dark street.

Had he detected a slight movement?

He'd loosed off a couple of shots before it dawned on him that in doing so he was revealing his presence. He drew back, cursing fluently. All he needed was a horse and he'd get away . . .

*   *   *

Tute's shots were closer than he knew, for Brad felt the wind of their passage past his cheek as he drew back into an alley between two adobe dwellings close by the factory.

But the risk had been worth his trouble, for at least now he knew where Tute was . . .

He peered round the corner at the dim outline of the factory. The gunflashes had come from what looked like a small office at the front of the building. From a nearby corral came the lowing of cattle now thoroughly disturbed by the firing.

Better let Tute know he was here; he lifted his *serape* and chanced a couple of shots at the office. The splintering of glass told him that although the range was long, his shooting was accurate.

The reply was immediate; three shots, accurately aimed, drove Brad back into the safety of the alley.

Brad heaved a sigh of relief. Now he knew for sure.

Tute was holed up inside the factory with no place to go!

* * *

Inside the office, Tute swore and drew back as a bullet whined past him. His armpits broke into a cold sweat. There was no way out except the way he came in. He was trapped. These damned rangers were everywhere . . .

He listened for a moment and, hearing no further noise, he turned round. Behind him was a door which he knew led into the working area. Maybe if he went in there he could make his escape through the doors in the loading-bay at the far end. From what he remembered, those doors were secured from the inside with a stout wooden post . . .

As he moved towards the inner door, he heard the splash of a footfall outside. In the gloom he could just detect the shadowy outline of the skinning-beds. Even though the floors were sluiced down each day, the smell of blood and offal seemed to hang in the air, making his stomach churn. He paused, holding the inner door ajar, narrowing his eyes as he waited for the outer door to open. As it did so, he snapped off a shot and slammed the inner door shut . . .

★　★　★

Brad held back, his Peacemaker held at high port. It was plain to see what had happened. The half-dressed night-watchman was lying on the floor of the office pole-axed, breathing stertorously. Tute's shot ricocheted off the metal door-handle with a shower of sparks before embedding itself in the wood. He didn't underestimate the reason for Tute's snapshot — it was to keep his head down while the outlaw put distance between them. Brad waited for a few moments while his night vision recovered from the brilliance of the sparks.

He pushed open the door slowly and entered the factory. A glimmer of the grey light of dawn was beginning to show through the windows set high in the walls.

Brad advanced slowly, all his senses alert. From his own scanty knowledge of these places, he figured there'd be an exit for the final products of what he considered to be the most wasteful industry in Texas, for the hides and tallow yielded from the cattle were mere by-products compared to the meat which was essentially wasted.

A slight noise attracted his attention. In the stillness of the factory the sound of a foul oath rang out. Brad smiled grimly. Tute must have barked his shins in his progress along the factory floor.

Better let the outlaw know he was still there. Brad steadied himself against a pile of hides and loosed off a speculative shot. He ducked low as Tute's riposte sent three slugs into the stockpile. The flashes were enough to tell Brad that the outlaw was now at the far end of the factory, probably somewhere near the area where the flesh was processed to render the fat. Bending low, he ghosted on tiptoe past the hide-beds, using the piles of hides as a screen until he judged he was three-quarters the way along the factory.

A scrabbling noise indicated Tute was doing exactly what he expected — trying to open the big double doors which led out of the loading-bay.

The light was strengthening by the minute now. The rain had ceased its drumming on the factory roof. Brad left the safety of the hides and made a dash for an area stacked with barrels. As he did so, Tute loosed off two shots, both of which passed close enough to make him glad it wasn't fully daylight. He crouched down low behind the barrels, peering into the gloom. Ahead lay a wagon, drawn into the bay ready to load the next consignment of barrels of tallow drawn from the vats. Tute was over by the door, struggling to lift the heavy wooden bar which secured it in place — a job which normally needed the united efforts of two men.

Brad took careful aim with his Peacemaker. Tute's lanky frame was a perfect target . . . but as he made to squeeze the trigger, Brad recalled Red Hall's stricture — no unnecessary killing . . .

Moving the weapon slightly to one side, he pulled the trigger. The slug missed Tute by a mere inch. The outlaw whirled round mouthing a stream of profanities.

'I'm giving you a chance to surrender, Tute!' Brad shouted. 'From where I am you're a sittin' duck. Throw down your weapon and come out nice an' slow.'

Tute swore again and as Brad dodged back behind the barrels, a stream of bullets pierced one. A thick mushy stream of tallow exuded through the splintered hoops and began to trickle slowly down the outside.

The factory fell silent again. The outlaw was using the respite to reload. For the first time, Brad began to have misgivings about his ability to carry out his lieutenant's orders to the letter.

He chanced a look round the barrels. The door was clear.

Where the hell was Tute?

A slight noise came from the direction of the wagon. Brad looked up to see Tute's upper body appear over the stack of barrels, gun in hand. Both men stared at each other in a moment of complete surprise before exchanging a volley of shots.

At the same moment from the far end of the factory there came the sound of men's voices . . .

Tute flung up his skeletal arms and gave a hoarse cry. Brad flattened himself against the stack of empty barrels, bringing several of them tumbling about his ears.

Half-stunned, he was vaguely aware of the sound of running feet and then a shout of 'I got him!'

Flinging a barrel aside, Brad rose to his feet to find himself confronted by his lieutenant.

'So I finally found you, Sergeant Saunders,' Hall said.

'Where's Tute?' Brad demanded. 'I had him holed up at this end of the factory.'

'Sure you did,' Hall said. 'Trying to handle everything on your own as usual.'

Something in his superior's tone gave

Brad the odd feeling he was amused about something.

'Hey, Brad, come on over here and take a look.'

It was Miller who called across to him.

Brad followed Hall past the wagon towards the tallow vats. Miller and three rangers were standing beside the lanky figure of Tute.

Brad's jaw dropped. 'What the hell . . . '

His exclamation was lost in the shout of laughter from the assembled rangers.

Tute was truly a slight to see. His pilfered pants finished half-way down his pole-thin calves, the sleeves of the shirt finished likewise down his bony forearms. But not only that, he was covered from head to toe with a thick layer of tallow-fat . . .

'Looks like he slipped and fell off the wagon into yonder vat.' Miller was leaning against the wagon, helpless with laughter. 'Lucky fer him the tallow hadn't set — it broke his landing.'

Brad's face broke into a slow smile.

The only person who didn't think it was funny was Jordan Tute . . .

'OK,' Hall snapped, bringing his men to order. 'While you've been pussyfootin' around with Tute, I've checked the place out. Neither Solomon nor Grimes is here in town.'

'So where are they, then?' Brad asked Tute.

'Go to hell!' Tute snarled.

'You may get there sooner than you think,' Hall said. 'Believe me, Tute, I promise you a rope is waiting just as soon as the judge pronounces the death sentence . . . '

Tute's face turned white.

' . . . unless of course you assist me in my enquiries,' Hall continued.

'You sayin' you'll put in a good word fer me?' Tute asked suspiciously.

Hall's eyebrows raised. 'I don't do deals, Tute. On the other hand the judge might take any help you offer into consideration . . . '

'Solomon's gone to Eli Greensbee's

ranch,' Tute burst out. 'He's aimin' to get even with Bannerman and take his wife hostage to rob the bank.'

'And Grimes?'

'He's disappeared, but I reckon he's gone to Dolores to look fer his kid brother.'

Hall exchanged glances with Brad.

'Looks like the wires got crossed,' he said.

'There's somethin' else you should know,' Tute said sullenly. 'Solomon had reckoned on meeting with us in Dolores at noon today.'

⋆　⋆　⋆

Grimes led his brothers out of Dolores on the trail which ran parallel with the county line and led north.

The events of the evening culminating in the killing of the two outlaws had shaken him. And despite hints from his brothers that they would prefer to find someplace to shelter from the pouring rain, he stubbornly refused to listen and set his horse to a steady mile-eating canter towards his intended goal.

Joel drew his horse alongside Zeke's. 'Why did he shoot those two guys?' he asked in a low voice. 'They helped me get away. I don't understand it.'

Zeke gave his brother a long sideways looks.

'Maybe you will some day — iffen you live long enough.'

'Where are we goin', Zeke? Why the all-fired hurry?'

'Shut-up, kid, you're asking a sight more questions than's good fer you.'

Four hours solid riding brought them to John Summers' ranch. The rain had stopped and Grimes signalled his brothers to stop and they removed their slickers.

'Ain't this the place we stopped by a coupla days back?' Curt asked curiously.

'Sure, I remember it,' Jud said. 'Guy here had a wife who was a real good-looker.'

As the pale moon showed fleetingly through the galloping rainclouds, the twins exchanged glances. Zeke was hunched forward in his saddle, Frank the same. Joel stared uncomprehendingly at the broad back of his brother.

Grimes tightened the straps holding his slicker in place and said, 'OK, boys, let's pay John Summers and his wife a visit.'

10

By commanding an extra horse per man, Lieutenant Hall, accompanied by Brad and eight rangers, was able to gallop back into Dolores an hour before midday.

They found the place in an uproar.

Hall and Brad left the men to care for the horses and headed for the Sheriff's Office where they found Cally with Bannerman.

The rain had gone, the sun was shining, and a warm breeze was blowing through the open door. Beyond it they could see the collapsed exterior wall of the cell.

'What happened?' Hall demanded.

Bannerman scratched his ear with his good hand. 'I still can't believe it,' he said. 'There's this thunderstorm an' I'm sittin' here mindin' my own business when suddenly there's this almighty crash an' the cell-wall caves in.'

'Was it an explosion?'

Bannerman shook his head. 'Nope — I know one of them when I hear one. I reckon the prisoners were tryin' to tunnel their way out an' the wall collapsed.'

'So they got away?' Hall said.

Bannerman nodded. 'It must have happened just as Grimes and his brothers arrived outside. Before I could move they had me roped up and lit out.'

'I found Lee here early this morning,' Cally explained.

'And you made no attempt to form a posse and give chase?' Hall demanded.

'He tried,' Cally said. 'But he was in no fit shape and the other deputies refused to turn out.'

'I did ride out a ways myself,' Bannerman admitted. 'A feller had reported findin' two bodies. I came across Quater and Moses. Both of 'em had been shot in the back.'

'By Grimes?'

Bannerman scratched his head. 'They rode out with him. Couldn't have been anyone else.'

Cally shuddered. 'Why would he do that?'

'Just fer the hell of it, I reckon,' Brad said sourly.

'But we have no witness and no proof,' Hall snapped. 'None of this speculation would stand up in a court of law.' He turned to Bannerman. 'Any idea which way Grimes was heading?'

'I prodded around awhile but I lost the trail. I ain't no tracker I'm afraid an' my shoulder was killin' me.'

'So they must have several hours' start,' Hall said. He turned to Brad. 'Take Miller and two men and get after them. I want Grimes and his brothers arrested and brought back here for trial.'

'But what about Solomon?' Brad protested. 'He's due here in less than an hour . . .'

'Don't worry about him,' Hall said grimly.

***

In less than an hour Brad and his men were in the saddle again. Brad was riding a hired horse, for Blaze needed a rest after his massive exertions of the last twenty-four hours. Miller rode alongside him with two other rangers, Marshall Taylor and Bill Gibson, tucking in behind.

They came to the outskirts of town, paused at a fork in the trail and cut sign.

'Guess they went thisaway,' Taylor said. He was a powerfully-built man who seldom spoke, but when he did his fellow rangers listened.

No-one questioned his judgment and they took the direction he indicated and kept riding, working as a team, checking out the sign continuously, their horses eating up the miles along the trail Brad recognized as the one leading towards the northern border of Vance County.

It was late afternoon when they

arrived at a small spread owned by Cal Weston, a man Brad had visited earlier on his tour of the border with Kell, Weston had spotted their approach and was waiting for them, one foot perched on the corral fence, when Brad and his men drew up in front of him.

'Howdy, Sergeant Saunders.'

'You seen any sign of Grimes lately?' Brad enquired.

Weston removed his pipe and spat non-committally.

'Iffen it's any help, he's quitting. Solomon's finished,' Brad said.

Weston hesitated.

'So you have seen him?'

Weston nodded. 'One of my boys says he saw him crossing my land early this morning headin' north towards John Summers' place.'

Brad nodded and cast an eye at the sun. 'If we take a short break we can make Summers' place before sunset.'

'What if Grimes ain't there?' Miller asked.

'Then we'll make camp and move on

in the morning.'

'You're welcome to a bite to eat,' Weston said.

He walked with Brad and his men across to the barn. After they had attended to the needs of their horses the rangers went inside and Mrs Weston served them bread, slices of beef and as many cups of coffee as they could drink.

Whilst they ate, Brad brought the rancher up to date with recent events.

'So your lieutenant wants 'em all arresting, does he?' Cal Weston mused, puffing his pipe. 'Seems a bit ambitious, don' it? I reckon he's tempting fate. Now Cap'n McNelly, he had the right idea — shoot first and ask questions afterwards. If I was in your shoes I wouldn't give a guy like Lucifer Grimes a chance to argue. No sirree, I wouldn't have no truck with this arrestin' business iffen I was you.'

'Hush your mouth, Cal Weston!' Belinda Weston scolded him. 'If you want to be any real help to Sergeant

Saunders, why don't you offer to ride along with him?'

As Cal Weston choked over his pipe, Brad drained his coffee-cup and rose to his feet.

'Thanks fer the offer, Mrs Weston but we're paid to do what we do.'

'Any special reason for Grimes to head this way?' Miller enquired of Brad when they hit the trail north again.

Miller's question jogged Brad's memory. What was it that John Summers' wife had said? Suddenly her words came to him with the force of a hammer-blow.

'*I didn't like the way he looked at me.*'

He went cold inside. A woman like Jane Summers didn't make remarks like that without good reason . . .

Miller's question remained unanswered as Brad spurred his horse into a gallop, and he and his men rode the remaining distance along the trail winding through the seemingly endless landscape of catclaw until the ranch-house came into view.

Brad reined in, took out his spyglass and focused it. The place seemed quiet enough. No doubt if things were normal, the Summers family would be having their evening meal. But a lifetime of coping with violent behaviour had given him a sixth-sense as far as trouble was concerned.

Several horses were stamping around in the corral. Near the doorway he picked up what look like a shapeless bundle lying on the ground. It took a moment or two before it registered that it was a corpse. He took a deep breath . . .

John Summers!

'Boys, you heard what the lieutenant said,' he muttered. 'We're supposed to arrest these guys. I'm gonna ride in alone and draw 'em outside. While I'm doin' that, spread out and cover me.'

'With respect, sergeant — no,' Gibson said quietly. 'If Grimes recognizes you, you could be in trouble. Far better if someone he doesn't know goes in first.'

When the others concurred, Brad didn't argue. Times had changed. McNelly himself never stifled initiative — the Ranger captain never regarded himself as the sole source of ideas, he was always willing to listen to suggestions from his men. And what was good enough for McNelly was good enough for Brad.

Suddenly, the sound of a woman's scream rent the air. It seemed to grow in power, reaching a crescendo before it attenuated into a choking sob.

'Christ Almighty!' Miller exclaimed. 'Who the hell was that?'

'Jane Summers!' Brad muttered under his breath. He looked at his men, his face set hard. 'Boys, if there's gunplay, I want first crack at Grimes.'

His companions nodded.

'OK, let's go.'

Gibson waited while Brad and the rest checked their Winchesters. On Brad's signal, the ranger spurred his horse forward and cantered up to the house.

As he drew near, a figure rose from the deep shade of the stoop.

'Hold it right there, mister.'

'Well, now, that ain't much of a welcome fer a guy who's stoppin' by,' Gibson replied. 'Say, would you be one of the Grimes brothers?'

The sound of a gun cocking alerted Brad.

'State your business, mister,' the man repeated. 'Otherwise you're liable to end up lying in the dirt alongside this fella.'

'What sort of question is that to a guy on the run?' Gibson protested.

'On the run, you say? Are you one of Solomon's men?'

'I was,' Gibson said. 'Until the rangers arrived.'

'Hey, Frank, quit talking to yourself,' a voice shouted tetchily from within.

'Ed, I gotta guy out here who's got news about Solomon,' Frank called back.

There was a scuffle and Brad gave a grunt of satisfaction as Grimes, followed by the rest of his brothers, emerged from the house. Grimes was pulling on his shirt, his gunbelt already fastened about his waist.

'Who's this?' he demanded.

Gibson played his part with all the aplomb of an accomplished actor. 'A company of rangers rode into Kell and took Tute prisoner. Then they came back to Dolores an' waylaid Solomon . . . he's finished.'

Grimes' eyes narrowed. 'Now wait a minute. How do you know that?'

'Because he's a ranger.'

Grimes twisted through forty-five degrees to look up at Brad seated on his horse. The outlaw and his men froze to a tableaux as they took in the unpleasant spectacle of the Winchesters held by Miller and Taylor and the pair of Peacemakers which had appeared in Gibson's hands faster than the blink of an eye.

'You and your brother are under arrest, Grimes,' Brad said.

As he spoke he prayed Grimes would draw. After what he'd done to Jane

Summers, to kill him in an act of self-defence would more than justify him in the eyes of his rangers. Even Hall could not deny him that . . .

Grimes' left hand was hovering menacingly over his holster for the crossdraw. The little group of men froze, each one of them knowing instinctively that the outcome of this confrontation would be resolved by the actions of their two leaders.

Suddenly Brad was aware of a blur of movement.

Christ, this guy's fast!

Realization hit Brad as his own hand reacted without any conscious effort on his part.

Both men's weapons exploded simultaneously with a roar of sound that made Brad's horse rear, squealing in terror. As he fought to regain control of the terrified animal, Brad became aware of burning pain in his left forearm.

The bastard outdrew me!

He was vaguely aware that the outlaw was toppling forward onto his knees.

232

Brad dismounted and approached Grimes. He had hit the outlaw in the shoulder but he was still holding his gun.

'You gotta choice,' Brad warned, holding his smoking weapon. 'Quit now while you're still alive.'

For a fleeting moment Grimes considered his options.

'You outdrew him, Lu!' It was young Joel who spoke, his scarcely broken voice sounding as incongruous as a cracked clarionet. 'If his horse hadn't bucked you'd have killed him . . .'

'Shut-up, kid,' his brother snarled. 'We ain't playin' games. If we tried anything now we'd all be dead before we drew another breath.'

From inside the house came the sound of a woman sobbing.

'Ain't you gonna do anything?' Joel shouted, looking round wildly at his brothers. When they did not respond, he dropped into a gunfighter's crouch.

'OK, Mister Ranger, let's see just how fast you really are,' he challenged

Brad with all the audacity of youth.

Brad's finger tightened a fraction around the trigger of his Peacemaker. In the back of his mind he could hear the quiet voice of Red Hall reminding him of his duty to take prisoners and abide by the law.

'Don't be a durn fool, boy,' he said quietly.

'You best listen, Joel, iffen you want to live,' Zeke said out of the corner of his mouth.

Slowly it dawned on Joel that his brothers weren't going to back him. Brad watched and waited, aware of the turmoil in his mind. Did every generation have to learn the hard way?

Grimes remained on his knees, his face pale, his mutilated hand clutching at his wounded shoulder, keeping as still as if he were carved out of stone.

'We're bested, Joel,' Zeke urged. 'These guys ain't gonna shoot us in cold blood. Let's take our chance with the law.'

Brad felt the tension drain away from

him as the outlaw slowly unbuckled his gunbelt and let it fall to the ground. His brothers followed suit, one by one, with Joel a reluctant last.

★ ★ ★

At noon precisely, Solomon and his men cantered into Dolores. Abigail looked neither right nor left as she rode close to her father. Both of them were surrounded by outlaws but the old man held his head high.

'Take courage, my child,' he said.

Abigail shrugged disconsolately. It was plain that it was all over. Earl was riding into Dolores unopposed, prancing and preening at the head of his men. The town was preternaturally quiet as though already lying prostrate at the feet of the conqueror.

'Where's Sergeant Saunders?' she muttered.

Her father shrugged. 'What can he do? He can only be in one place at a time. The age of miracles has long since gone.'

Solomon reined in beside the only hotel in Dolores.

'Only the best for my wife,' he said with a sneer at her father.

He dismounted and assisted Abigail to do likewise with an exaggerated flourish.

'I'll take the best room,' he ordered the lobby-clerk.

He turned back to Abigail. 'Now, my dear, how about you go and get some rest while your father and I visit the bank? I'll leave one of my men here to protect you.'

Abigail opened her mouth to protest but her father spoke first. 'Do as he says, my child.'

Abigail realized she had no choice but to agree. Solomon left her at the hotel and went to rejoin the rest of his men.

'Any sign of Grimes or Tute?' Solomon demanded.

'No boss, they must have got delayed,' Noah Cropper replied.

Solomon remounted his horse and

led his men in the direction of the bank. Once outside, he and his men dismounted.

'OK, boys, I got me one hell of a thirst. Noah, you take the old man inside. Don't bother with coins, go for the notes and bonds. Me, I'm gonna have a few beers in yonder saloon. Let me know as soon as you've done.'

'OK, boss.'

Solomon strode across the empty street, spurs jingling, and entered the saloon facing the bank. The place was empty apart from a group of men playing cards.

'Beer,' Solomon said, dropping a silver dollar in front of the barman.

'Sure thing, Mr Solomon.'

Solomon swallowed a long draught from the brimming glass and swaggered across to the card-tables.

'Mind if I sit in?' he asked mildly.

'Help yourself,' one of the men replied.

Solomon brought out a long cigar, clipped off the end with a silver cutter, lit it and blew out a stream of smoke as he studied the hand dealt to him.

This was the life!

Suddenly he tensed as something cold and hard jabbed painfully into the nape of his neck.

'What the hell!' he exclaimed.

'Take it easy,' a voice said.

Solomon turned slowly round to face the barrel of a Peacemaker.

'Who the hell are you?' he demanded.

'Lieutenant Lee Hall, Texas Rangers. You're under arrest.'

*   *   *

Early the following afternoon, Brad and his men escorted the Grimes brothers into Dolores. They had buried John Summers and on the way they stopped by to leave the cruelly-violated Jane Weston with her children in the care of the Weston family.

Words of Grimes' capture spread ahead of them like a prairie fire and on their arrival the townsfolk, emboldened by the presence of the rangers, lined the sidewalk to hurl such vile insults that Brad was compelled to order his men to draw their weapons and hold them at bay.

Lieutenant Hall emerged from the sheriff's office to greet them.

'Glad to see you brought them here in one piece, Sergeant Saunders,' Hall said ironically as his eyes picked out the bloodstained sling supporting the arm of the sullen-faced Grimes.

'I ain't, that's fer sure,' Brad growled. 'After what this guy's done he's damned lucky to be alive.'

Hall's affable expression changed.

'Better come into the office, sergeant.'

On the way in, Cally eyed his bandaged arm with concern.

'It's only a scratch,' Brad told her.

Hall listened in silence as Brad made his report.

'Well, Sergeant Saunders,' he said. 'I guess you did a good job under extreme provocation.'

If the lieutenant suspected that Brad had tried to force a showdown with Grimes, he didn't show it.

'That don't make me feel any better,' Brad replied. 'I was sorely tempted to finish the job there and then. After what Grimes did, McNelly wouldn't have argued about it, that's fer sure.'

'Maybe not,' Hall agreed. 'But unless we can establish a genuine system of law and order, nothing will change. And if the law is to be treated with respect it must be seen to operate through the courts and not by summary justice. I reckon we've got enough evidence to put the Grimes brothers away for a very long time. Grimes himself and Solomon will certainly hang, and Tute as well I reckon.'

'Providing we can get witnesses to testify,' Brad replied.

* * *

Justice Bligh returned to Dolores late that afternoon. A courtly, smiling

Virginian who had lost a leg at Shiloh, Brad was not deceived by his manner for he knew that underneath the veneer of politeness lay an iron resolve.

Bligh advised Hall that despite the lack of witnesses for their current criminal activities, the bench-warrants filed already against the Grimes brothers and Jordan Tute were such that he recommended their immediate removal to the respective counties where they had been issued. Hall wasted no time in implementing this at the expense of depleting his small force by half to escort the wagon especially adapted to carry the prisoners.

Joel Grimes was released into the custody of Eli Greensbee who agreed to employ him. Brad felt that Judge Bligh's decision was very perceptive. The defeat and capture of his brothers had so demoralized the boy it was clear he'd learned a hard lesson.

The case against Solomon was not so easy to justify. Hall was holding him under a round-the-clock guard using a room inside the courthouse as a make-shift cell.

'Bligh says nothing will stick unless I get witnesses to testify against him,' he told Brad. 'Our boys over in Kell haven't had any luck — Solomon has always been astute enough to get others to do his dirty work for him. He was playing cards when I arrested him, while his men were attempting to rob the bank.'

'Folks here in Dolores are wondering what we're playing at,' Brad said ruefully. 'They all know Solomon's the spider at the centre of the web.'

Hall sent Brad and Miller out to scour both counties for witnesses to testify against Solomon, but after a week they came back empty-handed. It was plain that his malignant influence was spread far and wide.

Brad wasn't in the least surprised when a dapper attorney sporting waxed moustaches and a silver-topped cane stepped off the stage and announced that he had sacrificed urgent and lucrative business in Austin in order to secure Solomon's immediate release. His manner was that of a man who considered he faced few obstacles in achieving that end.

In the meantime the townsfolk turned out in force for Tex Logan's funeral. Eli Greensbee attended along with Abigail. It was the first time Brad had seen her since he'd taken her out to the Diamond A.

Brad and Bannerman stood close by Cally's elbow as the preacher took the simple service of interment. She was brave, she didn't cry, but she held tightly onto both of them as four rangers lowered the coffin slowly into the grave.

'If Lieutenant Hall ain't careful, Solomon's gonna walk away scot-free, and we'll be back where we started,' Brad muttered to Miller afterwards as they relaxed in a saloon over a beer.

'You heard the latest?' Miller said. 'Solomon's attorney has rung the bell on Lee Bannerman. Turns out his real name is John Lascelles.'

Brad stared. 'The guy who outdrew Jerry Quinn?'

Miller nodded. 'That's the one. He did us all a favour, I reckon. After my investigation I can't understand why the case against him was ever allowed to stay on the file. As it is, Hall's had no option but to arrest him.'

'I don't believe it!' Brad exclaimed. He thought for a moment. 'D'you reckon this attorney's after doing some kinda deal?'

'You mean drop the case against Solomon an' let Bannerman go free? That's distortin' justice a mite, ain't it? Bligh would never agree to that.'

A shadow fell across the two rangers as the vast bulk of the shirt-sleeved pot-bellied barman loomed over them.

'Beggin' your pardon, Sergeant Saunders but Mrs Solomon has sent a message that she'd like to speak with you.'

Brad drained his glass and parted company with Miller. As he edged through the batwings and out onto the sidewalk he saw Abigail waiting for him. She looked pale and wan — but that was only to be expected.

'I just heard about Lee's arrest,' she said as Brad fell into step alongside her.

'Ain't nothing I can do about that,' he said. 'He's on our Wanted list.'

'But he helped you defend the bank!' Abigail exclaimed. 'Doesn't that count for anything?'

'It ought to, but it's outa my hands I'm afraid. Now as far as your husband is concerned, suspicion is one thing, proof is what we need — and that's hard to come by.'

Abigail hesitated. 'Brad, you know Earl's my second husband?'

He gave a curt nod.

'My first husband, Ben, was Earl's business-partner. He ran the ranch and Earl managed the hide and tallow factory . . .'

'So?'

'Well, one day Lee Bannerman found Ben's body in the barn. He'd been

245

strangled to death.'

'And you married Earl?' Brad said, fighting to keep the incredulity out of his voice.

Abigail nodded. She hung her head. 'It was a mistake. My father told me so. But I was left on my own with a ranch to run. Earl gave no indication of what he was really like. Marrying him seemed the right thing to do.'

'But if your father objected, why didn't you listen to him?'

'It was instinct, I suppose. He couldn't produce any good reason as far as I could see. But that's the way my father always works over lending people money.'

'A hunch, eh?'

Abigail nodded ruefully. 'And he's always right.'

'Just where is this conversation leadin', Mrs Solomon?' Brad asked gently.

They went inside the sheriff's office. From round the back came the clink of a stone-mason's hammer as men worked to repair the wall of the jail.

'I have proof that Earl murdered Ben,' Abigail said.

Brad stared at her.

'Back at the Crown Ranch I have a servant-girl called Peach. I had been aware for some time that her attitude towards me was well . . . odd, to say the least. Why, I did not know, until I discovered one night that she was with Earl. That's why I left with Lee Bannerman. But don't get the wrong idea, I've got no feelin' for him, I've made that clear.'

When Brad refrained from commenting, she continued, 'Peach arrived in town on the stage yesterday. She came to explain that Earl forced her against her will. Now she is expecting his child.'

'I'm afraid that's her word against his,' Brad said.

'She says she came upon Earl as he was strangling Ben in the barn. Earl threatened to kill her if she said anything. He made her spy on me. She was too frightened to do anything other than what he said.'

'Is she willing to testify?'

Abigail nodded.

'Then we've got him!'

Abigail drew a deep breath. 'There's a problem, I'm afraid — you see, she's a mulatto.'

Brad fished in his breast pocket for his Durham sack.

'So I can't see a jury taking Peach's word against Earl's,' Abigail voiced his thoughts.

He nodded. A long and bitter civil war had been fought, but the battle against racial prejudice could take generations to win . . .

'There's only one way out,' he said slowly.

Abigail faced him, her head held high. 'I know. I'll have to testify I saw Earl with her.'

Brad lit his cigarette. They paused as a buckboard trotted past.

'You don't have to do it,' he said. 'It'd mean dragging your private life through the courts. And you must know that a wife can't be compelled to testify against her husband.'

'Husband?' Abigail said scornfully. 'What kinda husband is Earl Solomon?'

*   *   *

'Think very carefully, Mrs Solomon. Are you sure you want to go through with this?' Justice Bligh asked when Brad and Lee Hall brought her to him.

'Someone has to make a stand,' she replied stonily. 'If my servant is willing to swear she saw Solomon murder Ben, that's good enough for me. After all, she's got nothing to gain by doing so.'

'Clearly an example that should be followed by a lot more people in Kell,' Bligh said. He turned to Lee Hall. 'Very well, I'll hold the trial immediately.'

*   *   *

Two days later, Earl Solomon, the would-be self-styled King of South-West Texas, was hanged in exactly the same spot where Brad had rescued Joel from the same fate.

There was no baying for blood this time; just a couple of hundred silent citizens witnessing the culmination of the due process of the law. The presence of the grim-faced Lee Hall and his heavily-armed rangers ensured that.

Afterwards Brad met Eli Greensbee outside the sheriff's office where he was talking in low tones with Lee Bannerman and Cally. Understandably, Abigail had remained at home at the Diamond A.

'Brad, Lieutenant Hall has confirmed that the charges against Lee are gonna be dropped,' Cally said. 'I know it's not his real name but somehow I can't call him John, he'll always be Lee as far as I'm concerned.'

Something in her voice made Brad stop and stare at her.

Bannerman cleared his throat nervously and his words finally came in a rush. 'Cally and me's gonna get married . . .'

'An' Mr Greensbee's gonna propose Lee fer sheriff. Ain't it wonderful!' Cally exclaimed, slipping her arm inside his.

Eli Greensbee caught the utter bewilderment in Brad's face.

'What are you going to do, Sergeant Saunders?'

'Me? I guess I'll be movin' on,' he replied.

THE END

A TOWN CALLED TROUBLESOME

John Dyson

Matt Matthews had carved his ranch out of the wild Wyoming frontier. But he had his troubles. The big blow of '86 was catastrophic, with dead beeves littering the plains, and the oncoming winter presaged worse. On top of this, a gang of desperadoes had moved into the Snake River valley, killing, raping and rustling. All Matt can do is to take on the killers single-handed. But will he escape the hail of lead?

THE WIND WAGON

Troy Howard

Sheriff Al Corning was as tough as they came and with his four seasoned deputies he kept the peace in Laramie — at least until the squatters came. To fend off starvation, the settlers took some cattle off the cowmen, including Jonas Lefler. A hard, unforgiving man, Lefler retaliated with lynchings. Things got worse when one of the squatters revealed he was a former Texas lawman — and no mean shooter. Could Sheriff Corning prevent further bloodshed?

CABEL

Paul K. McAfee

Josh Cabel returned home from the Civil War to find his family all murdered by rioting members of Quantrill's band. The hunt for the killers led Josh to Colorado City where, after months of searching, he finally settled down to work on a ranch nearby. He saved the life of an Indian, who led him to a cache of weapons waiting for Sitting Bull's attack on the Whites. His involvement threw Cabel into grave danger. When the final confrontation came, who had the fastest — and deadlier — draw?

RIVERBOAT

Alan C. Porter

When Rufus Blake died he was found to be carrying a gold bar from a Confederate gold shipment that had disappeared twenty years before. This inspires Wes Hardiman and Ben Travis to swap horse and trail for a riverboat, the *River Queen*, on the Mississippi, in an effort to find the missing gold. Cord Duval is set on destroying the *River Queen* and he has the power and the gunmen to do it. Guns blaze as Hardiman and Travis attempt to unravel the mystery and stay alive.